Seven Stories

Jane Roberts Wood

Seven Stories

De Golyer Library
Southern Methodist University / Dallas

Grateful acknowledgement is made to the following
for permission to reprint previously published material:

"Beneath the Jacaranda" in *Out of Dallas: 14 Stories*, edited by Donna Gormly,
Sally Schrup, and Jane Roberts Wood (Denton: University of North Texas Press
and the Dallas County Community College District, 1989).

"The Moon, with Love," *Pawn Review*, vol. 5 (1981-1982).

"My Mother Had a Maid," *Southwest Review*, vol. 83, no. 1 (1998).

Book design by Kellye Sanford

First edition
ISBN 978-1-878516-94-7
Printed in the United States of America
10 9 8 7 6 5 4 3 2 1

For Allien Eliza and Joshua Morris Parsons,
my dear mother and father

Contents

Foreword

Jane Roberts Wood, the acclaimed author of six novels, is a Texas treasure. With the publication of the seven short stories in this volume, Wood adds to her oeuvre. She brings to her novels and short stories sensitivity, authenticity, precision. Her six novels (*The Train to Estelline, A Place Called Sweet Shrub, Dance a Little Longer, Grace, Roseborough,* and *Out the Summerhill Road*) and her imaginative children's tale called *Mocha* attracted critical acclaim and robust sales and a loyal cadre of readers. The seven stories of this collection show Wood's gift for compression even as they show her range.

Wood's short story "My Mother Had a Maid," published originally by *Southwest Review* and honored as the best short story of the year by the Texas Institute of Letters, joins six others in this collection: "Flannery's Last Peacock," "Spurs That Jangle," "Beneath the Jacaranda," "The Moon, With Love," "Olive," and "The Dress." Each of these stories is a gem, and combined they represent a major contribution to Texas literature and culture.

There is a strong sense of place in the short fiction of Jane

Roberts Wood. She knows the Texas landscape intimately and incorporates nature, music, folklore, speech patterns, and values of rural life and small towns in her stories. Wood has an unerring gift for language and a keen eye for detail. Her stories in the collection have the ring of truth of character and situation. Throughout the collection, there is an emphasis on family relationships with all of their complexities and conflicts. From the narrative of a young man telling the story of his mother and her maid, a story of controlled horror; to the tale of a child dealing with many levels of estrangement and hostility and clinging to a surrogate mother for a sense of security; to a complicated double lovers' triangle and story of unrequited love and compelled duty; to marginalized country folk—a vagrant thief and an outcast girl with a past, linked for a moment in a search for beauty that is lost through carelessness; to the longing of an outcast family seeking and not gaining acceptance; to a curious and enigmatic episode of natural beauty and display of the body and freedom from constraint—a classical tableau come to life; to the psychologically distant but physically close relationship of two sisters who share a house but not a life and come to a moment of truth about the past that only intensifies their separation, these stories examine character and situation with precision.

Wood is a virtuoso of narrative technique. She succeeds in "My Mother Had a Maid" in presenting the voice of a man reflecting on events of his youth that lead to the dissolution of family unity and a violent death in the household. In "The Dress," Wood offers a narrative from the point of view of a dependent child unable to alter the circumstances of her life as she clings to the occasional stability and recognition offered by a kind caregiver. The first person narration in "Olive" allows the character Katherine to share with the reader years of conflicted love and duty and to portray a gallery of personalities who are investors in the plot. The narrators in each of the stories tell their stories candidly and tenderly.

In all of the stories of the collection, there is a striving for understanding, a quest for beauty, a desire for belonging, a search for love. The stories have ambiguity and call upon the reader to fill in information and interpretation. For example, in "The Moon, With Love," the reader is left to determine the paternity of the expected child or whether indeed there is a pregnancy. Wood is not a formulaic author who settles all questions; she is one who leaves open many possibilities for the audience. These qualities invite the reader to participate in the story, to engage in an active way with the narrative. Even with all the conflict and compromise set out in the stories, love and beauty abound and lead to affirmation and redemption. Like the acclaimed novels of Jane Roberts Wood, these stories add to the legacy of Wood and the canon of Texas literature.

PHYLLIS BRIDGES, PH.D.
Cornaro Professor of English
Texas Woman's University

Seven Stories

Flannery's Last Peacock

Beauty is a calling on the soul . . .
S. T. COLERIDGE

Duffy was a thief, and he traveled from one small town to another because of it. His face was lined by wind and weather, and if he had a worry it didn't weigh on him enough to line his brow. The straw hat he wore was stylish and made cheerful by a blue jay's feather stuck in the black band. On his back he carried a bulky, faded, navy-blue backpack. His shoes were as heavy as boots and laced to his ankles.

Duffy's hobby was repairs. He could fix anything—a leaky sink, a frayed electric wire, a sagging gate. A day or two with Duffy on the job brought a house to life again. But the repair business was empty of thrills. Fixing a sagging gate or a leaking roof did not cause the adrenaline surges to which he was addicted. Duffy liked poring over maps in order to minutely examine the neighborhoods of offices or houses he planned to burglarize. He loved hunting for jewels hidden in cof-

fee canisters or unused heating vents. And he was an artist
when it came to finding a good market for stolen goods. Duffy
would have been a brilliant detective had he not chosen the less
travelled road, so to speak. Simply put, Duffy was born to the
adventure of thievery, from Texas to Georgia.

Today, Duffy had followed a gravel road since daybreak
toward a place called Ponder. At mid-morning he had taken a
short cut through a dry corn patch and then through a field of
cotton, not likely to make it. Around noon, seeking shade, he
crawled through a barbed wire fence and walked into a pine
forest. After a hundred yards or so, he stopped in the coolness
of the piney woods to take a warm drink from his canteen.

And in the three seconds it took him to stow the canteen,
Duffy was flabbergasted by a tombstone that sent shivers down
his spine. It was a monumental, black granite grave marker.
Towering over him, it sat smack dab in the middle of the forest.
Out of respect, he took off his hat and stood there, marveling.
The tombstone was brand spanking new and fit for a governor
and not another marker around. Anywhere. No wife of, child of,
mother of. Just Joshua Morris. Born 1766. Died 1856. That only.
And it on a new grave. Now here was a sign. Duffy took note of
signs, and, not knowing what to make of this one, he stood fan-
ning himself with his hat. Now why would a man, dead over a
hundred years, be buried all alone and in a new grave?

He ran his hand over the granite and over the inscription
as well, thinking to puzzle it out. The wind lifted, and alongside the scent of pine needles warmed by the sun, there came
the heady, dizzying incense of money. He took a deep breath
and like a bee drunk from a honeysuckle's nectar he fell to the

ground, stretched out on the coolness of the grave, put his hat over his face and went to sleep.

All of a sudden, the warning light in his head turned itself on. Knowing better than to open his eyes, he lay still. Whatever watched him was strange. He felt it by the shadow it cast and the break in the wind. Relieved, he took a breath, and when he heard a stomping and a snorting, he opened one eye no more than a slit.

It was a girl he saw, standing on one foot, her left foot scratching the ankle of the foot she stood on. Her right hand rested on the head of a Jersey cow any man would be proud to steal.

Duffy slowly sat up and rose to his feet. He put his hat over his heart and made a slight bow.

The girl gazed at him. He glimpsed the tip of a pink tongue. She gathered what was inside her mouth and out came a pink bubble. When it retreated into the small cave of her mouth, she smiled. Her teeth were small and white and even.

He caught the scent of peppermint. The wind shifted. The cow snorted and pawed up dust.

"Needs milking," she said.

The cow's udders were indeed swollen and appeared to be leaking, a leak he had no intention of attempting to repair.

"If you've got a name, may I have it?"

She tilted her head sideways, considering his request. Her eyes were round and as green as emeralds.

"My name's Duffy. Duffy Duffield," he offered.

She lifted her right shoulder. "So?" her shoulder said. Then, with a graceful wave of her hand, she gestured toward the monument. "This here is my great, great, great grandpa," she said.

The formality of the introduction together with the sweetness of her voice caught him off guard. Verging on skinny, the girl stood tall, a good three or four inches taller than he. And she was adorned with gold. From an eyebrow, her ears, her nose, piercings glimmered and danced. Her jelled, spiked yellow hair shot golden rays into the sky. He caught a whiff of money again.

She tilted her head and leaned toward him. "Did you ever see a peacock?" He tried to remember. "No. I've seen pictures of them. No." He settled on that. "No," he said again.

"Well," she took a deep breath. Her round eyes grew rounder. "We got one," she whispered. "And it's the prettiest thing you ever saw. Real beautiful."

"Ah, a thing of beauty."

The scent of money was stronger. He took a deep breath. The girl's piercings alone would fetch a pretty penny. He was sure of it. And where there was that much gold glittering in the middle of a forest, there was bound to be more behind it.

The girl crossed her arms and leaned on the tombstone. A bird warbled. "Mockingbird," she said. Without blinking, she studied his face.

"Your family has a peacock?" he asked.

"No. Ponder's got one."

A triumphant "ha!" came from her throat. She smiled widely. "If he's in the middle of the street when a car comes, he'll turn his back on the car. Pecking along, he pays it no mind whatsoever. If a car honks, hurrying him, he'll spread his gold and purple and green tail feathers, and they are this wide!" she said, holding her arms straight out. "Wide as a car." Thrusting her palms forward, fingers spread wide, she whispered, "All of a sudden there's a thousand eyes!"

"Lord, have mercy!" he cried.

Her green eyes glimmered. She put her hand over her heart.

"The sight of it would stop a Greyhound bus. The car will stop, and the folks will put their heads out the window to see the peacock. Sometimes, the kids in the car will beat on the sides of the car. Rude!" she declared.

"Then it flies?"

"Hardly ever. He just pecks along the street until he takes a notion to leave."

She was calmer now, as calm as the peacock sounded, pecking its way across the street.

"Then it might be he sees something or hears something, and he'll fold his tail feathers and run. He doesn't fly much, except to roost. When the sun goes down, he flies into the big magnolia tree between the post office and the jail. That's where he sleeps."

Duffy felt the passion of curiosity. There was all that gold standing close. There was the expensive monument. And he had never seen a peacock up close.

"If you're going to Ponder, may I walk along with you?" he asked. "I'd like to see your peacock."

"Sure. It's close to sundown now, and he'll be going to roost pretty soon. I'll just bet you've never seen the likes of it!"

She turned to lead the way. The rope, binding the girl to the cow, hung limply between them as she accommodated her pace to the cow's. When the undergrowth allowed, he walked by her side in order to guess what her name was. He was pretty good at guessing names, especially the names of dogs. *Black* for black dogs, *King* for big dogs, *Shep* for German shepherds and if a dog had a spot, *Spot.* Guessing the name of this sylph-like girl with a voice as soft as a feather would be difficult. *Feather.* If he were naming her, that's what he'd call her. The name would suit her. But naming her Feather would call for a high quotient of the imagination, the kind he doubted Ponder had. With all that gold she could be called *Goldie.* No. She wasn't a material girl, despite her piercings. An old-fashioned song came to mind.

He whistled a few bars of it and said, "I'll bet your name is Jeanie."

Glancing over her shoulder, her eyes sparkled and her mouth quivered into a smile. It was a game. She was teasing him. Now she quickened her pace. Falling behind her and the cow, he failed to dodge a flick of the cow's tail that barely missed his eye but stung his cheek.

"Damn it," he said, dropping farther behind.

The girl chuckled.

She seemed to be leading him deeper and deeper into the forest. With each step he took, the woods grew darker. Duffy liked little towns, but this was a forest. You could get lost in a forest. Lose your bearings. Walking down a slight incline, he heard the sounds of rushing water, a lot of water. Duffy couldn't swim. He cleared his throat. When they neared the water's edge, he stopped short and saw with some relief that the water was so shallow the marbled pebbles in the creek seemed to float. Five small turtles in graduated sizes lay on an old log, half in and half out of the water. A leaf fell from a cottonwood tree and was swept downstream. A green snake doctor hovered over the water grasses near his shoes.

Suddenly, the girl's feet left the ground. "Jump!" she called and landed on the opposite bank. Then a soft clucking sound came from deep in her throat. "C'mon, Bessie. C'mon. C'mon."

Obediently, the cow ventured into the water. Halfway across, Bessie stopped, lowered her head and with her black nostrils flaring, took a long, quiet drink from the stream.

"Mr. Duffield?" the girl crooned. "C'mon. C'mon."

A Siren's call.

He made it across except for his left foot that splashed into the creek. Surprisingly, that felt bracing. As the three climbed the hill on the other side of the creek, the trees thinned and the sky lightened. He took off his hat and replaced it at a jaunty angle. When they reached the top, he saw the cluster of houses nestled in the little valley below.

"It's pretty," she said.

"Indeed it is," he said heartily.

They began their descent. It was steep. The cow and the girl, as sure-footed as mountain goats, ignored his slipping and sliding and grabbing hold of bushes to stay upright. When they reached the road, "This here's Main Street," she said. Well, he could have guessed that. "A little ways down the road, that's Ponder."

He felt a twinge of irritation. The walk to Ponder had been longer and hotter than he had expected. But, still, there was the strong possibility of money. The promise of it sharpened his senses and set him to thinking.

"Uh, Miss whatever your name is, I was just wondering why

your great, great, great grandfather is buried in a new grave."

"Well'um, he had a safe full of gold, and when he died folks never found the safe. They kept digging him up to find the gold that was buried with him. They finally had to move him to a new grave 'cause of the digging."

His intuition had been correct. There was gold here, somewhere. All he had to do was find it. Whistling "I Dream of Jeanie," he followed the girl along a worn path in front of the faded houses scattered along the main street. Head held high, hips barely swaying, she walked like a dancer. He took note of the straggly bushes, the drooping verbena, the yellowing wild moss, the faded hollyhocks. Nothing here felt like money. But, he told himself, in places like Ponder, folks don't spend money to fertilize flower beds.

Now the girl opened a sagging gate and turned the cow into the yard of a newly painted, yellow house with dark blue shutters. "This here's Granny's," she announced.

The cow bellowed mournfully.

"I got to milk her. You go on in and meet Granny. She might take a liking to you." When he hesitated, "Go on," she urged.

He watched the two disappear around the corner of the house. Then he tapped on the door. There was no answer. He tapped again. Still, no answer. Gingerly, he pushed the door open. "Hello, anybody home?"

"You're welcome to come on in."

The voice sounded like the girl's, lightly touching the rs, but deeper. Stepping inside, he saw that an old woman sat in a rocking chair in front of an open window. Her lap was magnanimous. The rest of her matched her lap.

Without turning her head, the woman said, "Where did she find you?"

"By her ancestor's grave."

"She brings home these strays."

Strays? Duffy straightened his shoulders. "Ma'am, I'm a repairman."

Suddenly conscious of the backpack he had worn throughout the day, he unfastened it and allowed it to slip to the floor with a clink and clatter.

The old woman looked straight ahead. "What's that?"

"My tools."

"And what can you repair, Mr. Repairman?"

"Everything. Anything, ma'am."

"Well, we got a leaky sink in the kitchen. You want to try your hand at that?"

She leaned from her chair and fumbled for a cane that lay just out of her reach. He picked up the cane. Feeling the richness of its carved ivory handle, "This is a mighty handsome cane," he said, placing it in her hand.

"It belonged to the girl's great-great-great-granddaddy," she said and, rising from her chair, she tapped the way into a kitchen brightened by rays from the setting sun.

The old lady was blind. She couldn't see a damn thing. He had stumbled into the wrong house. Nothing here was worth stealing. Wrong house. Wrong town. He took off his hat and prepared to bid the lost day and everything that had filled it farewell when the girl, carrying a bucket of milk, came in the back door.

"Granny, this here's Mr. Duffield. I'm sorry, Granny, but

we have to hurry. He'll be crossing the street, and Mr. Duffield wants to see him."

The girl leaned forward, kissed her granny's cheek and was gone, leaving the screen door flapping.

The old woman shook her head. "That peacock will be the death of her yet. She's just too crazy about it. After Miss Flannery died, her peacocks took to the wild. People couldn't catch them, and what with foxes and guns and bobcats. . . . Well, you know." She pushed the milk bucket aside and, fumblingly, picked up a potato and began to scrub it. A smile crossed her face. "Somehow this one made its way all the way over here from Milledgeville. Folks say it's her last peacock."

Before Duffy could respond, the girl stuck her head in the door. "Mr. Duffield, hurry! Come on! C'mon. C'mon."

Oh, lordy, her voice was pure.

Since he was here he might as well take a look at the peacock. Abandoning his backpack, he hurried out the door. The girl was already a half a block ahead of him, her hair ablaze in the sunset, by the time he reached the gate.

Three doors down, a small, brown woman, sitting in a porch swing, called, "You better hurry, girl. You gonna miss the show."

Girl. That seemed to be her name.

A man in shirtsleeves and wearing a hat came toward them. Tipping his hat, he stepped aside to allow them to pass.

"You coming, Mr. Buchanan?" she asked.

"Naw, I'll just set on the porch and watch the traffic pile up when he crosses."

She picked up her pace, lengthened her stride. He trotted to catch up. A half a block ahead, he saw that two men leaned against the brick wall of Sam's Feed and Seed Store. Printed in small, red letters below, he read: *Heifers for sale. One bull.*

The feed store bricks needed pointing. He was good at that. And when the time came, there was sure to be a cash register in the store. Catching up with the girl, he kept his eyes on the men. When he and the girl were almost even with them, they stepped out into the middle of the walkway, blocking their passage. Hands on his hips, the short, stocky one crossed his arms, looked at them and grinned. His nose was wide, his lips thin, his hair in a skinny ponytail. The other man was tall, thin and swarthy. Mean looking. The kind who'd have a switchblade in his boot. On his tee shirt were the words: *My take home pay won't take me home.*

The men shifted their positions so that their arms rested lightly across each others' shoulders.

"Why hello there, Guinevere," the stocky one said. "Who you got with you? He your new boyfriend?"

Guinevere. Duffy never could have guessed it. *Rumpelstiltskin* would have been easier.

"Shut up, Ralph. Standing there grinning like a toad. I ain't got a boyfriend. Don't want one."

"Come on now, Guinevere," Ralph said. "He from out-of-town? What you charging him?"

Impervious, imperturbable, Guinevere took Duffy's hand. "Come on, Mr. Duffy. There's a bench for us to sit on, right by Sam's front door."

The swarthy one put his hands on Guinevere's shoulders.

"Leon! Take your hands off me. Get out of our way! I mean it!"

"You heard the lady," Duffy said, and instantly felt a dangerous jolt of his heart. Thinking to forestall a heart attack, he put his hand over his chest and breathed slowly.

Looking at Duffy, Leon narrowed his eyes and thrust out his chin. "Now who in the hell do you think you are!" he growled.

"I'm this lady's guardian," Duffy said gamely and broke into a cold sweat.

All the while grinning and winking at Duffy, Leon put his hand behind Guinevere's neck and pulled her face close to his. "Sweetie, I got five bucks. You gonna spread your legs for that tonight?"

In one swift movement, the girl knocked Leon's hand away, broke off a crepe myrtle branch and began flailing the men about their faces and shoulders as they cowered, laughing, in their frenzied efforts to protect themselves.

He was into it now. Any minute, the men would come to their senses and beat the tar out of him. But before he could decide whether to apologize or run, she tossed the branch aside.

"Pay them no mind," Guinevere said calmly. "C'mon. Let's go sit down."

When they had settled on the bench, his heart slowed so he could get his bearings. Across the street, he saw the peacock's roost—a dark green, shiny magnolia that grew between the barred windows of the jail and the flag-bedecked post office.

A man who looked like Ralph walked briskly across the street and, ceremoniously, began to lower the flag. The man *was* Ralph! Now Leon, wearing an orange vest and the serious face of a traffic cop, stepped to the curb and stood at attention.

He turned to ask Guinevere about their sudden transformation into citizenship when, behind them, the door of the feed store opened, and a man stuck his head out. "Girl, I thought you might not make it tonight."

"Sam, you know I wouldn't miss it. This here's Mr. Duffy," she said, and to Duffy, "The feed store belongs to Sam."

Duffy stood and held out his hand. After shaking it, Sam took up a position behind the bench. Guinevere put her finger to her lips. "Sh-h-h-h-h. He'll be coming along now."

Sitting by Guinevere on a hard bench in a strange little town, the idea came that the two of them were sitting together in a kind of Quaker silence. Being a man who abhorred violence, Duffy found the idea a comfort.

Leon stepped out into the street and held up his hand. A black Ford screeched to a stop. From the other direction a brown pickup came to a more leisurely stop. The peacock tentatively, gingerly stepped into view, and Duffy knew his expectations had been too high. The only unusual thing about the peacock was its size. Other than being as big as a Thanksgiving turkey, it was ordinary, a scrawny thing you wouldn't turn around twice to look at.

Wondering how much a live peacock would bring, or for that matter, a single feather, Duffy leaned back to observe the people standing up and down the street, watching the peacock. He felt pretty certain the zoo in Atlanta would pay a pretty penny for the last peacock.

Then Guinevere sighed. And, oh, Guinevere! Sweet Guinevere! Her sigh was the richest sound of pleasure and pure joy Duffy had ever heard. Never had he been able to call a sound like that from any woman he had ever slept with. He turned to look at Guinevere and saw a face suffused with wonder. Bewildered, he turned to look again at the source of

Guinevere's ecstasy. The ratty-looking peacock, ignoring the traffic cop and the braking cars and the people watching, had begun to peck its way toward the other side of the road. The town was crazy. The girl was crazy. And he was a fool.

Then she touched his arm, and, oh! how to describe it? Before his eyes the iridescent colors of a sultan's cloak—the dazzling colors of the greenest green, the richest gold, the deepest purple—opened and spread and grew. He blinked, blinked again, and saw the splendor, the glory of the feathers. Then he saw the thousand eyes!

"Dear God!" he whispered.

As the peacock neared its roost, it stopped and slowly pirouetted. Leon stepped back to allow a single lane of traffic to pass and, at just that instant, Duffy saw a red pickup speed toward the open lane, swerve, brake, and roar away leaving a swirl of feathers lifting and drifting in the stunned silence of the evening air.

And now Guinevere was screaming, "No! No!" and sobbing and burying her head in her hands.

Horrified, unable to believe any of it, Duffy slowly stood up and sat down again. He watched Leon drop his orange vest in the middle of the street and saw Ralph walk back across the street to raise the flag to half mast. Sam brought a tow sack and began to gather the feathers. Leon plucked a feather from his shoulder and dropped it into the sack, picked another one from the awning over the feed store and deposited it.

Guinevere lifted her tear-streaked face to Duffy's. "I want every feather," she said sternly. And when Duffy had walked up and down Main Street to find every last one, she took the tow sack in her arms. "Let's go home," she said.

All night long Duffy walked the street of Ponder. The town was too much and too crazy. Too unreal. He was worn to a frazzle. There was too much emotion here. He disliked a crying woman above anything else on earth. In fact, he hated crying women. He disdained faded houses and sagging fences. It was time to return to his real profession. Past time. He had to set his sights higher. Make up for lost time. He had always wanted to rob a jewelry store. And if not now, when? Ponder didn't have one, but Atlanta had hundreds. He would take what he could get from Ponder and begin planning to rob a jewelry store. The operation would be complex, but he relished the challenge.

By morning he still felt hung over, but he had come to his senses. By the time Guinevere handed him a glass of warm milk and fried a couple of eggs for his breakfast, he had settled on his next step. By mid-morning he had fixed the gate and the leaky faucet. Then he began on the roof. About noon she handed him a bologna sandwich and a Dr. Pepper, and, together, they sat on the back porch steps for lunch.

Wearing a mournful gray blouse and skirt, she listened as he began to unfurl his plan. "My work here is finished, but before I leave. . . . Now Guinevere, this is what I've been thinking: You need closure on your peacock's demise."

"What's that?" she said.

"Closure. Some way to help you get over it. Fast."

"What's demise?"

"Death."

She nodded, picked up a stick and began to draw a feather in the dirt.

"I think the feathers ought to be buried."

Frowning, she studied the tow sack slumped beside the kitchen steps.

"I think they ought to be put in the ground where your great-great-great grandpa's buried. Sacred ground, so to speak."

"You do?" she said doubtfully. "I thought maybe a fan."

"Guinevere, peacock fans are a dime a dozen."

"That's true."

"This was her last peacock."

"And the prettiest."

He glanced at the sky and saw the gathering of thunder clouds. "Looks like we might get some rain," he said. "We'd better get started."

In little more than an hour, with his backpack and a shovel over his shoulders, they arrived at the grave. He marked off what would be a narrow grave and began to dig. When he had finished, Guinevere tenderly placed the tow sack in the grave and stood looking down at it. She clasped her hands together as her tears fell on the tow sack. Slowly she began to rake the dirt in over it.

When she had finished, he took her arm. "I have to leave tonight. I have to get back to work."

"You do?"

"Before I leave I want to say something important to you."

"What?" A shadow passed over her face.

"Let's sit here for a minute," he said, taking a jacket from his backpack and spreading it on the pine needles near the grave. Taking her hand in his, he said, "Sit down."

Looking intently at his face, she sank lightly to the ground.

He sat cross-legged in front of her and, again, took her hand in his. "The thing is I've noticed there are some who don't treat you like the lady you are."

Smiling, she ducked her head. "Mr. Duffield, I ain't no lady."

This persuasion might take longer than he had thought. Duffy leaned back on his hands. If he wasn't averse to violence, he would take the piercings by force. He cleared his throat. "Guinevere, you are a lady. More than that, you are a lady who needs no adornment. Your emerald eyes, your golden hair, your royal manner—this is all the adornment you need."

Every word he spoke was the truth. He knew it was. It was all true.

She drew her knees close to her chest and fingered her spiked hair. "I've been thinking of letting it grow."

They watched a crow settle on the gravestone, shake its shiny black feathers, peck at the stone. Guinevere smiled and held out her hand. "C'mere, c'mere," she said. The crow cawed and flew away.

"Letting what grow?" he asked.

"My hair."

Rays of the setting sun spread across the sky, high-lighting her spiked hair with faint tinges of pink and orange. He wondered how she would look with longer hair. Impatiently, he pushed aside all thoughts about the girl's hair. He had planned to be on the road long before dark, and here it was almost dark and he was sitting by a skinny girl in a solitary cemetery. Briskly, he sat up straight and crossed his legs in front, Indian style again.

"Exactly. Good idea. Let it grow. Now, about your piercings. You don't need them. The fact is they detract from the real you. Guinevere, you have a queen's name," he said passionately. "A queen would never wear piercings. I think the piercings should be buried with the feathers."

"Buried! Mr. Duffield, that's crazy. I wouldn't think of burying them!" She began to finger each one, as if making sure it was still in place.

"Well, I am at a loss now. I can't help you," he said coldly.

He stood and picked up his backpack. He would have to move on. Atlanta was waiting. The biggest mistake he had ever made was to run up on a crazy girl with a leaky cow. Now, cow-like, she was chewing on a pine needle.

She took the pine needle from her mouth. "I've been thinking of selling them."

Glory, hallelujah! He felt like shouting it. "Oh, Guinevere, you're right. It would be better to sell them. Now as to a good market . . . ."

But she was already taking them off, taking them out, releasing each one and dropping it into his outstretched hand. "Sell them," she said. Pulling up her blouse, she removed a single stone, as sparkling and green as her eyes, from her navel and handed it over. "I don't care about wearing them anymore."

"I'll find the best market. I'll do that. You know I will."

She shrugged her shoulders. Without the piercings, he saw that her face now seemed to go to points. The shadows under her eyes were dark-green bruises.

"I have to go home, Mr. Duffield," she said dully. "Bessie needs milking. Granny worries."

How could he have ever thought a voice that grated was like a song? Wearing the gray dress, the battered hiking shoes, she trudged ahead. The saucy, spiked hair looked out of place on the drab girl who climbed the hill ahead of him. The sylph-like creature of his imagination had been replaced by reality.

By the time they reached the pot-holed road, Ponder had gone to sleep. He caught up with Guinevere and forged ahead. When they reached Main Street, "I can hitch a ride on this corner," he said, anxious to be rid of her.

"Will you be coming back this way? Someday, you'll probably come through here again, won't you? Maybe someday?"

"I doubt it. I've got some pretty complicated affairs to take care of."

She had never been the girl he thought she was. He felt betrayed by her and by the town. He saw that the clouds that had promised rain had instead brought a thick fog that roiled and swirled through Ponder, transforming it into a forlorn, shadowy place. The figures that came toward them appeared to step out of the gloom and, in a few steps, disappear into it. A man coming slowly toward them seemed wraithlike until he cleared his throat and spat tobacco juice into the middle of the street.

"Sorry about the peacock," he muttered when he passed them.

An old eighteen wheeler, lights ablaze, hove noisily into town. Duffy stepped into the street with his thumb up. Brakes screeching, the truck ground to a stop.

"Where you going, Mac?"

"Whichever way you're headed, Buddy."

Glancing at the girl, he saw that she looked spent. Dazed.

"Goodbye, Guinevere," he said, and with his eyes fixed on the future, he climbed up into the cab and, thankfully, sank into the seat.

He hadn't realized how tired he was. He slept. Woke. Dozed again.

"Man, you're done tuckered out," the trucker growled. "You must have had some weekend."

"Yep, but I'll get over it."

He slept again. And after two cups of coffee, he felt alert enough to plan. He could walk into any jewelry store from Atlanta to El Paso and steal a bracelet, a bracelet that would take a woman's breath away. But not Guinevere's. Guinevere liked peacocks.

He sighed. Deeply. A new idea popped into his head and fluttered around there until he became attached to it. Cheered by the idea, he began to whistle.

"I can do without the noise," the trucker said, but after a few minutes of silence, "What's that you were whistling?"

"It's an old Irish tune called 'I Like to Live Simple and Airy.'"

"Well, don't we all," the trucker grumbled.

Duffy drifted off again and, dreaming, heard, "C'mon. C'mon, Mr. Duffield. Jump!" And Guinevere was suddenly before him, real as day. Adorned with her piercings, her hair glittering and gleaming in the starlight, she stood looking over her shoulder at him, chuckling. He groaned.

"What's up, Mac."

"A girl," Duffy answered, feeling in his pocket to be sure the piercings were safe.

"A girl will do it," the trucker growled. "Go back to sleep. I was enjoying the peace and quiet."

He thought to tell the trucker about her, but how could you explain a tall skinny girl with a leaky cow. Instead, he said, "Did you ever see a peacock?"

"Aw, man. That's the craziest question I've ever been asked. How would I know?"

"You'd know, Buddy. If you ever saw one, you'd know it."

Outside Atlanta, the trucker pulled into a truck stop next to a load of cattle. Powerful, aromatic smells of hide, sweat, cow dung, and pine swept over Duffy, conjuring up images of Ponder nestled in the little valley and of Guinevere, gleaming and glistening and sweet talking, while the two of them sat and waited for a peacock to peck its way across Main Street.

The trucker was picking up speed. "We'll be in Atlanta before midnight," he said.

"Now you're talking, Buddy!" said Duffy.

His next job was shiningly clear to him. All he needed was a tow sack. Maybe wire cutters. "A peacock is the prettiest thing," he said. "A thing of beauty."

"Man, you're crazy."

Duffy rolled down his window and thumped the outside of the truck. "Buddy," he said, grinning, "I guess maybe I am."

Beneath the Jacaranda

Although John welcomed the telephone's ring that interrupted the quiet in his office, his wife called so seldom that it took a minute for him to recognize her voice.

"Can you come home? Right this minute?" she was saying now. "I want you to see with your own eyes what's going on in the Carlyle's front yard! I can't believe it!"

"What's the matter? What is it?" John asked.

"I can't tell you over the phone, John. And you wouldn't believe me if I did. But it's the neighbors. You'll just have to see it for yourself! It just beats all!"

Fumbling for his car keys, John pushed his chair back from his desk and hurried out the door. Never in the past five years of his diminishing practice had Louise called him home from work. Long before his Dallas office had become almost empty of clients, she had let him know that he was not welcome in his house during the day. "Poor Mary Elizabeth," she'd say, "Larry stays home all day. Underfoot!" spitting out the word, tossing it out as carelessly as one would toss a cat out the back door. Or, when Melvin Kusin retired, "Poor Dolores. How would Melvin feel if Dolores had plopped herself down in the middle of his law office all day long? Why, with Melvin underfoot, Dolores can't get one thing done."

Oh, how fervently he'd agreed with Louise in those days. Under Louise's foot was the place he would least prefer to be. But then he had never dreamed that as the neighborhood young people grew up and moved away, their dogs and cats, growing old and dying, would not be replaced. "We're just waiting for the last kid to leave home and the cat to die," Fred had chortled only last Friday. "Then Marjorie and I are going to pack our bags and travel!" Fred then hitched up his pants and drove a ball straight down the fairway for a par on the first hole at Bent Tree.

Once or twice a month the screech of tires on the pavement outside John's office signaled a need for his services, and he always treated these injured animals. Two dogs were in the clinic now; a German shepherd, recovering from over four hours of surgery on a fractured hip, and a little female schnauzer, old and in shock. The dogs' tags identified the owner but his telephone messages and notes to the address had gone unanswered.

Now, leaving his office, he felt a surge of surprise that Louise needed him at home. And always as he drove through the white crepe myrtle bordering his drive, he remembered his youthful longing to paint their soft whiteness, remembered the first time he'd seen them, the night he had moved into the house with his first wife, Molly. That night, they had walked along the drive, marveling at the brightness of the white flowers in the moonlight. "They're beautiful," she murmured, "a

kind of purity made visible. John, you'll have to paint them!"
But he never had.

He swung his car smoothly into the garage, close beside
Louise's new Lexus and, moving as quickly as his one hundred
and sixty pounds would allow, he went through the garage, into
the garden room, and up the two steps into the living room.

Louise stood with her back to him, looking through the
French windows toward the ground just across the street.
"Look!" she said, thrusting a pair of binoculars into his hand.
"Just look," and she pointed to the two-story Georgian house
directly across the street.

John focused on the stone archway that marked the entrance to the Carlyle's property. Each leaf of the ivy that climbed
and trailed, softening the stones, could be seen as clearly as if
it lay on his breakfast plate. Suddenly aware of Louise's heavy
breathing, he glanced briefly in her direction. She held one
hand to her abdomen and the other over her right breast, pro-
tecting her vital organs from the view for which John now
searched. He searched the driveway slowly, moved up the steps
to the old stone porch. "Where?" he asked softly.

"Under the jacaranda," Louise whispered.

Blurring the front porch, the elms, slowing just past the
giant oak, he focused on the bright green, fern-like leaves that
nestled blue flowers, flowers like smoky spumes of color. He
followed the branches down the trunk of the tree, growing
snug up against the master bedroom. And there, mother-of-
God, under the jacaranda, sat Betsy Carlyle! Nude!

Shakily, slowly, he exhaled a pent-up breath. "Well," he
said. Clumsily, he laid the binoculars on the window seat.

"Well, now," he said again, easing himself onto the window seat beside the binoculars.

"John, I think we'd better call somebody. After all, if Betsy's taken leave of her senses, we had better call her husband. Or an ambulance. Maybe we'd better just call an ambulance." One of the most unsettling things about Louise was that when she was upset, her voice flew off in all directions, and this last flight, begun in a hissing whisper, ended in a wobbly soprano. She picked up the binoculars and, leaning forward, put one knee on the window seat to steady her gaze. "Well, she could be drunk. I've never known Betsy to drink much, but still . . . maybe we just ought to call the police." She finished in a high-pitched nasal whine.

John took the binoculars from his wife and brought them again to his eyes. In full bloom, the tree's buttercup blue flowers floated against the stones of the house, soared up against the blue of the sky. And a white butterfly, an early cabbage probably, danced alongside the blue blossoms. The pitch of Louise's voice faded for a minute and rose again as she continued her monologue. " . . . if Trevor is even in town. John, isn't this the worse thing you've ever seen? You'd better call Trevor, and when you do be calm. Just tell him he'd better come home and see about his wife. It is very, very, very important to be calm. We don't want any trouble in the neighborhood."

John looked at Louise, at her pink furry house shoes, her blue velvet robe that was beginning to sag (Louise never dressed until after her afternoon nap), her mouth which seemed always pursed for chanting: *Underfoot. Underfoot. Underfoot.* He saw that not even the unexpected sight of Betsy's nudity had brought a sparkle to Louise's flat, brown eyes.

"Louise," he said quietly, "for God's sake. Shut up." If he heard her gasp, her sobs, her footsteps as she ran upstairs to her bedroom and slammed the door, he gave no sign of it. He went into the kitchen and, for the first time he could remember, he poured himself a drink in the middle of a working day. He took it neat. Most things do break. Words not heard since college days, came, unbidden, into his mind, admonishing him as he carefully replaced the bottle on the shelf and resumed his place in the window seat. Again he took up the binoculars. Betsy's body was golden against the dark trunk of the tree. Her face was serene. He moved the binoculars to her neck. Did he only imagine a pulse beating there? Over her breasts, tracing her arms clasped loosely around her knees. Everything—the sky and branches, the blossoms and stones, the nude woman, the butterfly, all coming together at just a single moment—created an astonishingly innocent landscape. The air poured into the room, air as fresh and crisp as a dog's nose. He longed to gather up the day and hold it. It had been years since he had picked up a brush, mixed paint upon a palette, but now his fingers tingled. Surprisingly, he felt a slight arousal. He took another drink and, laying aside his binoculars, he gazed at the beauty that had blossomed across the street.

Thus, John did not see Marcie McGuire's car as it slowed and swung into the drive next door to the Carlyles' house. Ordinarily, Marcie McGuire, the baby sitter, would have helped the three English children out of the car, rung the doorbell of their grandmother's house, and waited until Ellen English came to the door to let them in. But today, just as the car turned the corner onto Maple Street, Marcie's five-year-old Timothy began to throw up, and all the while Marcie was helping the younger children out of the car and shepherding them along the walk and up the steps to their grandmother's door, she could hear Timothy alternately retching and sobbing. Hastily, she pushed the doorbell, told the children good-bye and hurried back to her own still heaving Timothy. Quickly backing the car out of the driveway, she was vaguely aware of the blue flowers on the tree next door, but she did not see the nude figure of Betsy Carlyle beneath it.

Their grandmother, Ellen English, always watched for her darlings, but at this minute she had plunged into the bottom of her over-the-shoulder bag to find her cell phone and call her son or, if he was out-of-pocket, Eunice, his wife, their very busy mother, to say that her car had refused to start and that it was already past the time that the children were scheduled to be dropped off at her house.

As the English children waited on the porch for their grandmother to come open the door, Nathaniel, one of the three-year-old twins, noticed a measuring worm on the azalea bush near the porch and squatted down to look at it. His twin shook her head. "No, Nathan. Bite you." Elizabeth's three years of accrued wisdom had taught her that everything, sooner or later, bit Nathan. The twin's four-year-old sister, Amy, looked at the front door and pushed the button again. When the door didn't open, she stuck her thumb in her mouth, and then her gaze fell on the tree next door. Amy loved blue, and she promptly marched down the steps and over to the Carlyle's yard for a closer look at the tree. Nathaniel and Elizabeth followed.

The three saw Betsy almost simultaneously, and what they saw was a lady sitting on the grass underneath a tree, a lady who looked very much like their mother when she took a bath. They stood in a semi-circle and looked at her unabashedly. Betsy looked back at them the way one looks at a summer shower or the first honeysuckle bloom or a mockingbird. Her eyes shown blue like two blossoms caught and held in midair on the way to the ground. And unlike other grown-ups, the lady asked nothing of them—not their names or how old they were. Not even where their mother was.

Three-year-old Elizabeth suddenly began to run toward the nude lady, her chubby legs flying, and when it looked as if she would run right into her, she stopped and sat squarely on the ground beside her. Solemnly, she looked at Betsy's foot, and she looked at her own. She took off one shoe and sock and wriggled her toes in the noonday sun. And then she took off her other shoe. She looked at Betsy's body and, quick as a wink, slipped her dress over her head. Then she sat down on the grass and scooted her panties off. She began to run in circles around and in and out of the shadows under the tree.

Nathaniel and Amy looked at the lady whose only response was a soft beatific gaze. Convinced, Nathaniel tossed his shoes to the ground, his socks toward the holly bush, and his shirt onto the lowest branch of the tree. By the time he hopped out of his shorts, Amy had joined the game, running in ever widening circles beneath the tree. Nathaniel, spying the sprinkler on the ground, changed the direction of his course long enough to follow the hose to the hydrant at the corner of the house and turn it on full force.

Water jetted, spiraling round the woman, up into the branches of the jacaranda, dripping from the ends of its fern-like fronds. In minutes, the water became a leafy waterfall through which the children ran, laughing and calling each other's names, their sturdy, wet bodies glistening as they ran in and out of patches of sunlight on the grass. To those of a fanciful nature, if any had happened by, it would have seemed that three fountain cherubs had suddenly come to life.

At this very moment, the children's mother, after a brief conversation with her mother-in-law, was driving anxiously toward Ellen's house. Her anxiety bordered on anger. Eunice hated for well-laid plans to go astray; hers seldom did. But this morning they had. The salmon mousse she had made the night before had not set up, and that meant that she would have to take a client out to dinner that evening. Her sitter had called to say Timothy was sick, and Eunice had no choice but to ask her mother-in-law whether the children could be dropped off at her house from nursery school. This alone meant a considerable loss of control, since she suspected that even though she had firmly forbidden it, her mother-in-law sometimes gave the children drinks containing both sugar and caffeine. Eunice much preferred to have David's parents visit them. "David, let's have them come for dinner," she was fond of saying. "That way we can have more control!" Control was one of Eunice's favorite words. She was an independent C.P.A. because she could control her work hours. And she had married a man, good-natured and bright, whom she could control.

And now, this morning, nothing was in order. Leaving her office in the middle of the day was out of the question. Ridiculous! And she had to do that very thing. Now all at once, and on top of all this, Eunice, turning in the drive of her mother-in-law's house, saw her children, as naked as the day they were born, frolicking in the twirling, spiraling, dripping water.

Then she saw Betsy Carlyle.

"Well, for goodness sakes," she said aloud. When Eunice was truly shocked she reverted to the oaths of her childhood, unconsciously foreswearing the "My Gods" and "Damns" of her adulthood. "Well, my goodness," she said again, "a nude woman!" She leaped from her car and lunged awkwardly across the lawn toward the mobile of cavorting children, dripping tree, and spiraling water—all seemingly emanating from the quiet, still figure of the woman at the center.

"Elizabeth! Nathaniel! Amy! Get in the car. Now!" Eunice shouted, scooping up shoes and socks, plucking one of Nathaniel's off the water hydrant. The children became as motionless as the woman, except that Amy's thumb moved to her mouth and Elizabeth's chin began to quiver. Nathaniel, having ducked around the other side of the jacaranda, was out of sight. Eunice looked at the wet bundle of clothes in her hands. Dazed, she realized she was wet and getting wetter. She hurried to the hydrant at the house's corner and turned the water off. Then she looked at Betsy Carlyle.

She thought the woman moved her head slightly, as if acknowledging Eunice's presence. Eunice looked into her face and her response to the order and calm she saw there was physical. Some comprehension—perhaps only momentary, of the complexity of Eunice's own life, of the contrast between it and the aura of response on the woman's face, this quiet, nude woman's demeanor—came to her, for Eunice dropped the sodden bundle of clothes to the ground and smoothed back a lock of dripping hair from the forehead.

What is all this fuss about? Betsy's blue eyes seemed to ask.

Eunice's answer tumbled out. "Oh, this morning's been too much! I have to take a client out to dinner tonight, and David said just last night that we had somehow lost our way, had taken the road most traveled, and Nathaniel stutters." Eunice, folding her arms defensively, paused for a breath. Then she put her hands on her hips. "Well, you're the one who's nude!" she said angrily. "You're out here in the middle of the day without a stitch on making me feel like a bad person!"

What Eunice heard then was a chuckle. Warm. Inviting her to laugh. And surprising herself, Eunice grinned. "I must have looked like a fool," she admitted. "Running around in circles. Grabbing wet clothes. Yelling. Look," she said, "can I get you anything? A raincoat? Maybe an umbrella?" Then Eunice laughed out loud. This surprised her even more. In school her reputation had been that of a wit, but she had, over the years, somehow mislaid it, and now, here it was, showing up again.

Eunice stood a minute, politely waiting for a response, but now Betsy Carlyle seemed to be looking off beyond Eunice's head, through the branches of the tree, as if Eunice had already left or had never been there. Uncertainly, Eunice gathered up the wet clothes and herded the children across the yard and into the car. She sat looking across the green of the St. Augustine grass to the jacaranda and the small, still figure of the woman beneath it. At this distance, although it could not have been more than sixty feet, the scene invited a mood of peaceful contemplation, and Eunice felt as she sometimes did in New York when, walking by an art gallery, her eyes would be drawn to a painting, usually a large landscape, prominently displayed, but in the far reaches of the room. She would often stand in the doorway a minute, enjoying it before walking on to her hotel or Elizabeth Arden's or Arthur Andersen's accounting offices. Now, suddenly and unaccountably, she felt eased, buoyant. She turned to look at her children, smiling at them over her shoulder.

"We'll stop on the way home," she told them, "for hamburgers and, maybe, a coke. Why we've got plenty of time for that," she said, as she drove away. Three minutes later, a green Mercedes, its tires squealing, rolled into the Carlyles' driveway.

Louise, using an antique cane she had bought in case her disc should ever slip, tapped the floor just above the window seat where John sat. "John, John," she called shrilly, accompanying her calls with resounding thumps.

He went to the foot of the steps. "I see him, Louise. You called Trevor didn't you?" he said accusingly. Then more kindly, "I suppose someone would have called in any case. Although, if Betsy Carlyle wants to sit nude in her own front yard, I don't see . . . ."

Louise interrupted John, overriding his words, trumpeting out a play-by-play description of the activity across the street. "Trevor's talking to Betsy now. Oh, poor man. He's begging her to come inside. Now he's shaking his finger at her. Now his fist. Oh! He's walking fast, almost running, now he is running, into the house. John, you missed the children. You missed all of that. Little heathens! Out there like little puppies. Now Trevor's coming outside again. He's walking like he's really mad. He's carrying a blanket."

To escape Louise's voice, John went back into the garden

room. He took out his pipe and lit it in the house, a thing he had
not dared in the eleven years he had been married to Louise.
Putting his pipe in his mouth and his hands in his pocket, he
looked across the street just as the blanket came down. His
throat felt tight and, as he massaged the left side of it, he felt
a tear slide down the side of his cheek. He watched as Trevor
wrapped the blanket around the struggling woman, watched
as he carried her into the house. Slumped on the window seat,
John wondered whether the shrill little cries he heard might
only have been the calls of a mockingbird.

The next day Betsy was gone.

That afternoon Trevor cut down the jacaranda tree.

The Moon, With Love

The moon was full that fourth day on the beach, full but skim-milk pale at dawn's first light, the morning of the last dog-fight between a Navy Corsair and a Japanese Zero. We had just taken Peleliu, one of the small islands. Peleliu was to be a stepping-stone to victory in our war against Japan, but for us it was a stepping-stone into a nightmare with over 200 of our own dead and 900 wounded. Although we had hit the beach hard, coming in on LSTs, by then the Japanese had learned to pull back fast, away from the support guns of the navy. After that first wrenching assault, there was almost no defense of the beach so only a small company of our "Wildcat" 81st Division was left behind to guard the rear, and I was one of them.

Although we had dug in at the edge of the jungle, Eddie and I lived on the beach. In those last days of the war, sensing the end was near, we came out of the jungle and we slept on the beach, watching the moon catch the topmost crest of each wave and feeling the softness of the sand and the wind and the quietness of the moon. For me, those three nights were a fragile bridge that began to span the blood and mutilation of the

last twenty months, the wounds made by that last necrophilic
assault of the very beach upon which we now slept, a bridge
that I sensed could take me back over the ocean to a country
(oh, how I believed this then) where life, where individual life,
would once again be sacred and intact. And during those three
long gentle nights when those of us who still lived waited for
peace, we talked, Eddie and I, about home. I told him about my
fourth grade teacher and the time I lost her goldfish down the
drain, and he described his aged high school Latin teacher, the
only "lady" he said he'd ever known. I wondered aloud about
my two-year old Jason whom I'd never seen and thought about
my girl-goddess, his mother. Those three soft nights, for the
first time in months, we dared to speak of home.

That fourth day I was, I think, still asleep and dreaming
when I heard the noise of the airplane engines, at first no more
than a buzz, like a worrisome mosquito too close to my ear.
Then I was awake, suddenly, all the way awake and by turning
my head only slightly, I could watch the aerobatic dance against
the moon, a dance made macabre by the beauty of the beach,
and the quiet softness became a loud whine as I watched, first
leaning on my elbow, then sitting up, and suddenly I was standing and Eddie was there too, and we were walking, Eddie and I,
to the edge of the water. We watched silently, and I longed with
the most startling anguish for this fight not to be happening.
Only three days away from the nightmare of taking this beach,
only hours away from seeing buddies randomly swatted dead,
I yearned desperately for the lives of those two unknown, un-
seen pilots. And then, the plane fell. It fell beyond the reach of
the first light of morning. And suddenly I was running, the
tips of my feet hitting the tips of the waves, then knee-deep

and running still, my body straining toward the downed pilot, driven by the soft breezes and the pale moon and the soft sand, and by a rediscovered reverence for a soul, already lost. I swam furiously and silently and hopelessly, swam until I could no longer lift my arms, until I could only turn on my back and let the tide take me back.

As I lay there on the beach, the memory of that hot night when I came to know the Sandbergs swept over me, and I knew it was because of them, because I had known this other family, that I swam out beyond the moon that morning, swam to give the dead flyer the life he'd already lost.

But that other night. Let me tell you about the town and about the Sandbergs and about the terrible wonder of that hot summer night in their backyard. The town is a small, East Texas town. It is the place where I grew up and to which I returned after World War II, and where I live still. In this small place the Sandbergs were the "others." Outside. Grotesque in their obesity, in their smell, their clannishness. Loathsome in their secretiveness. In a town that accepted the dangerous whoring of Dixie Lee's mother (I had seen her nude myself, hunkered down, hiding behind her bedroom door); the habitual drunkenness of old man Taylor who was as often as not passed out in the alley behind our house and who would, on occasion, grab a child's ankle, chortling gleefully, and hold it a minute before releasing the child to run home terrified to his mother; the consummate goodness of the rabbi (a saint's life is more suspect than most) who looked steadily out at the town through those dark, intelligent, brooding eyes; in a town that accepted all of these, the Sandbergs were despised and despising. Oh and Claire. Our beautiful Richard Cory who had been

graduated *summa cum laude* from Harvard, had come back
home and had never gone out again, who had *never gone out*,
but, instead, had had his groceries and his laundry delivered,
and, later on, the stereo system parts he himself assembled,
delivered. In the seventies, of course, it was and is the computers that occupy his time. Even Claire, once our beautiful young
boy, now oddly old, broom-sticked with his ill-assorted clothes
hanging on, his face pole-thin, his grey hair long and sparse,
but still a sweet man and Mac, who owns the corner grocery,
says that when the ox is in the ditch, and he himself delivers
the groceries, there Claire might be whistling and playing with
his computers, never glancing around, but even so always polite and our town's own genius. Certainly Claire is one of us.
Our attitude toward these few who are markedly different has
always been one of caring and acceptance, an acceptance that
comes in a small town because we know these special ones,
have always known them.

But in all the town I alone, only I knew the Sandbergs. I
know them still.

On Sundays, Mr. Sandberg would drive his wife and his
daughter to the cafeteria and double-park. Then he'd hobble
around on his little feet, made small by the gelatinous flesh that
ballooned about them, and he would reach into the blackness
of his long black Buick and slowly ease first Mrs. Sandberg and
then Maxine out into the hot, white sun that is Cold Springs
on a summer's Sunday. By then the after-church cafeteria line
would be coiled inside and trailing out the door along the glass
front of the building, sometimes reaching almost to the corner. Like visitants at the carnival side show, we would watch

the unloading from our place in line, catching furtive glimpses of the monolithic bodies made exotic by the darkness of their skin and the brightness of their clothes, but never daring to look into their faces, to risk meeting their eyes as if the knowledge that might then come would be too terrible to hear. And they, these three Sandbergs, were as indifferent to us and as unaware of our presence as a locust to his empty shell. The three would stand there, black eyes blinking, mouths gaping open, recovering from the terrible heaving effort of leaving the car and climbing the steps to the sidewalk. As they passed to wait inside "for the line to go down," I would look carefully away, but always I glimpsed the shiny, black hair that fell in thick waves to the women's waists, and smelled the earthy odor of their unwashed bodies.

On Saturdays I delivered for Mr. Sandberg's feed and seed store in Sandflat. Away from his family, moving slowly down the aisle of his store, stopping to straighten the Shirley Temple blue cereal bowls (one free for every purchase of Day and Night Salve), stacking the feed catalogues on the shelf, carefully dipping and weighing the Bermuda grass seed from the wooden bin, and without the presence of the other two, he seemed fully human.

"How're you doing in Latin, son?" he'd growl, and I'd say, "Not too good, sir." Then he'd give me a list of deliveries, twenty-five cents for each bicycle delivery, fifteen cents if I used the truck. I'd make as much as five or six dollars on a Saturday.

Then it was June, and leaving The Hut on Saturday night with Dixie Lee, I backed into Howard Payne's car to the tune of one hundred and twenty-nine dollars. Howard called to say that Chance-Moore was fixing the car, and they'd send the bill to me. My dad just said, "Richard, I think you'd better pay that bill before you take the car out again."

On Monday, I stopped by Dixie's on my way home. "I thought we'd go to the graduation dance together, but you haven't asked me and Bill Lawson has," she said. I was desperate. I wanted to take Dixie and take her in Dad's car. Dixie could play boogie-woogie, jitterbug all night long, and she made me laugh.

"So what's one hundred and twenty-nine dollars to an expert bicycle rider like you? You ride faster backward than I can ride forward," she giggled, her long, brown hair swinging, hips swinging too, below a waist I could reach around with two hands. She handed me a plate of brownies and a frosted Coke, and I knew I had to get the money to fix Dad's car. Somehow, I had to take her to the dance. Never mind that there were sometimes men there with her mother (once I saw a man cut up and lying with blood-soaked bandages in the bedroom), I wanted to be with Dixie every minute.

On Saturday I went back to Mr. Sandberg's office. I told him about my accident, said I'd come early, stay late, work afternoons unpacking orders, straightening shelves, sweeping out, said I'd do anything if he would advance me the money. He leaned back in his swivel chair, and his stomach tilted upward. He moved one hip to the left and the other to the right and when he had balanced his stomach, he crossed his hands over it, his gold belt buckle glittering through his fingers.

"Well, son, there is something," and he stopped, took out a cigar, clipped it, lit it, took a long drag, and looked away over my head toward the front of the store. "Maxine needs some help with her Latin, and if you could come out to the house a couple of evenings a week for a while, say on Mondays and Thursdays, I could . . . . "

I was astonished by what I was hearing. Maxine was Miss Amos's star pupil. Sitting at her desk, her presence made formidable by her huge size, she seemed unaware of Miss Amos and of the rest of us, but when no one in the room could respond, Miss Amos would say, "Maxine?" and she would smoothly translate the Latin into poetic, lucid English. "I sing of the arms and the man," her liquid, bell-like voice would sound, "And of the hero who first from the shores of Troy . . . ." Then the rest of us, given this momentary reprieve, would go on to the next passage to see if we could make some sense of it.

The shock I felt at Mr. Sandberg's suggestion must have been clearly visible because he said nothing more for a long moment and then, "Think about it, Richard," and he stood up and moved ponderously out into the store.

All weekend I stayed at home in my room, hating the Sandbergs. Dixie. Myself. But Monday afternoon I went to the feed store. "I'll be there tonight," I said, and Mr. Sandberg opened the cash drawer and counted out ten, ten-dollar bills, two fives, and nineteen ones.

That night after school I asked my dad for the car. "I'm working for Mr. Sandberg for a couple of nights a week," I told him.

I don't think anybody knew just where the Sandbergs lived, and, for sure, I had only the vaguest idea. Grateful for the gathering twilight, I drove out Arkansas Lane and turned left past Fielder Park, and started checking names on the mailboxes. The houses got farther apart, and the road more narrow until, finally, I came to a dead-end and was about to turn around when I saw the house. A great dark mass made grotesque by the silhouettes of the trees that grew around it, as isolated from the town as the Sandbergs, it seemed to me the only place they could have lived. There was no mailbox at the end of the drive, no lights coming from inside the house, but a bright, white light came from behind it, delineating the house.

I sat there for a minute, fooling with the car keys in the ignition, turning the switch off and on, off and on. God, I wanted to leave, to turn around and get out of there! Only the thought of the money already paid made me ease the car door open and begin the long journey to the Sandbergs. With the wind up a little, the pines made more noise than I. And moving carefully along the walk, I eased up the porch steps to the front door. I was about to ring the doorbell, when sounds of a door slamming, a voice calling, stayed my hand. Clearly, the noise was coming from the back, and I went back down the porch steps, headed toward the light. There a thick and ancient hedge grew as high as my head, but at its base the heavy old stalks left small triangular openings, and I knelt down to these and crawled until I could see into the yard.

A world such as I'd never before seen sprang up from the darkness, a world lit by candles and oil lamps and a dazzling string of multi-colored electric Christmas lights. Into the middle of this came Maxine, barefooted, wearing a white blouse and a long, full, white skirt. The yard was embowered (then I did not know the word, but what other is there for such extravagant profusion?) by masses of roses, snapdragons, black-eyed Susans, daisies, and hollyhocks, their pale white blossoms like small moons scattered about the yard. My eyes were drinking in the wild array of color—among the flowers a red cloth on a picnic table, a yellow hammock strung between two magnolia trees, their white blooms like white bowls; my nostrils were assaulted by the smells of meat and onions cooking, garlic and chocolate, aromatic smells mixed together, a potpourri of scents; and my ears by a panorama of sounds—cats meowing, dogs barking, and growling, and the *gssssfs, gssssfs, gssssfs* chatterings of a monkey! All those animals! In those depression-ridden days, I had never known anyone who could afford the luxury of feeding more than one or two animals table scraps.

A great jug of wine was on the table and to this Maxine came striding as at that moment from the outer perimeter of darkness came the crisp click of hooves, and across the terrace, the stone terrace, trotted a little white goat. Mr. Sandberg, stretched out in a chaise lounge by the charcoal grill, playfully grabbed one horn as it trotted by. If I'd been taken up and set down in another world, in another age, I could not have been more astonished. The generosity of the scene, its magnificence, was overwhelming.

"Princess, Princess, Princess," like a hoarse gull Mr. Sandberg called, "let me pour you a glass," and with surprising agility he was up and pouring and handing the glass to his daughter with a flourish.

"Papa, he's not coming. I don't care. But, he's not coming!"

"Princess, these small pale boys in this small, pale town. These young anemics. Either he comes or he doesn't! He is not for you. Sit, sit," and he pulled a chair forward and gently, oh how many times I'd seen this act of devotion, he eased her great bulk into a chair. Then he picked up a guitar from the picnic table and strummed a few chords.

"Mama," he called, "come out. I've poured the wine. Come out!"

And Mrs. Sandberg in a red blouse, wearing a long black skirt, came down the steps, stepping around a duck that ran along by her side until she sat in the white porch swing, whereupon it jumped to the seat beside her and, tucking its feet under, slowly settled as if to its nest.

Then I'd never seen a Rubens or a Brueghel or heard the lush dissonance of Bartok, but I must have imagined them or perhaps I'd only yearned for a richer, more opulent life. The scene before me satisfied old yearnings I had never known before. Maxine was in profile now. Sitting silently in her chair with her long straight nose, her mass of black curly hair, her dark eyes (their great black orbs clearly visible), she seemed a part of this opulent night, a pagan goddess.

Suddenly a cry of anguish, a lone wail, rising above the clattering of animals, shattered the night. "Papa, Papa, he's not coming!"

Knowing I was the subject of her sorrow, expressed with the same exuberant extravagance with which the yard was filled, I hugged the ground, afraid to breathe, but feeling as if I must stay there forever. Surprised by the new emotions the exotic scene provoked, I felt as if all my life had been lived in a desert, and I had now come to a green, fertile jungle only to find it filled with sorrow. I had never seen my mother cry, had only seen her dab at her eyes with a handkerchief before rushing quietly off to her bedroom, and so these racking sobs I now heard released some tightness I had always felt. A rapt onlooker, I was so caught up in the scene before me that I lost all sense of self.

Now Mr. Sandberg knelt by her chair, and he no longer seemed grotesque, only lost, lost and sad. He took her hand in his, patting it tenderly.

"Princess, I will do everything for you. You know I will. What do you want? I'll get it. What do you want most in this world?"

And Maxine made a little bell-like sound and leaning forward, she threw her hands up and out. "The moon, Papa! I want the moon!" she cried. And she began to weep again, proudly, making little gasping sounds without covering her face or lowering her head.

Mr. Sandberg looked at her, patted her hands once again and rose to his feet. He walked to the center of the yard and stood looking at the moon.

"Such a little thing for a princess to want," he said. He drank the last of the wine from the glass and tossed it aside. "Well, I'll give you the moon." And then Mr. Sandberg jumped! He gave a little leap upward, no more than three inches off the ground. And Maxine's voice, sounding like the tolling of all the bells in the world, came again, "Jump, Papa! Jump for the moon!"

And with tremendous effort, he again pushed himself away from the earth, "Again Papa! Jump again," she cried.

"Papa," Mrs. Sandberg called, "You've lost your senses. Maxine, stop him! Stop your papa!" But neither of them heard her.

"Jump, Papa! Oh, I want the moon," would come her anguished cry. And he would stand there gripping his fists, looking only at the moon, and then he would jump, his labored breathing clearly heard above the excited barking of the dogs, the quickened *gsssfs* of the monkey, the shrill bleating of the goat. With the perspiration pouring from his body, he jumped. Again and again he jumped. And in this exotic setting, his unbelievably awkward little hops seemed somehow heroic, and I found myself leaning forward, hoping against all hope that he could get the moon, that he could give his beautiful princess what she wanted.

He fell finally. When he could no longer lift his arms, he fell to the ground, and he sobbed hopelessly for his beautiful, sad princess. And I slipped away.

Tuesday I returned the money to Mr. Sandberg. "She knows more Latin than I do," was all I said. But as I stood in the cafeteria line the next Sunday, I looked into their eyes, and as Maxine swept by I nodded my homage to a princess.

Some years later, home on Christmas leave, I heard that Maxine had had a baby. My mother said the talk was that the baby had been fathered by a hitchhiking bum who had stopped in town only long enough to earn some money delivering for Mr. Sandberg. Dixie said that no, it was not the hitchhiker's baby, that he'd never gone out to the Sandberg's house, and besides, he hadn't stayed in town long enough. She leaned over the table at The Hut and whispered, "It's Mr. Sandberg's. Everybody in town knows it is!"

"No," I said. "Mr. Sandberg's not the father."

"How do you know? What makes you so sure?"

"I know," I said. "I know it's not his baby." And more than that I would not say, for how could I explain to Dixie that who the father was did not matter, that what mattered was that somehow Mr. Sandberg had found a way to give a princess the moon?

I've never forgotten that other family. In the richest times of my life that indescribably beautiful, sad scene, that great-hearted man's longing to give his daughter the moon, comes floating back. When I swam to save the pilot, already dead, when my own daughter was born, when her black-haired head crowned, in all the richest moments of my life, that night comes floating back, strangely insistent, laden with love and with anguish.

The Dress

"Annie Ruth. Annie Ruth." Daddy is trying to whisper. "Annie Ruth!" His breath is warm on my ear. "Your momma's sick. I'm taking you to Mrs. House's. Come on, honey. Put your arms round my neck. Come on, sweetie. Let's go." I want to sleep, to put my nose in the middle of the pillow, my thumb in my mouth and sleep. Momma does not want me to suck my thumb. "Little Sister," she says. "I know you're behind that door, sucking your thumb. Big girl like you. Ought to be ashamed of yourself. Come out right now!"

The door flies back and instead of its smooth, hard comfort, her face is there. Blue eyes staring. Wrinkles in her forehead and fingers ready to pinch. My mother never spanks. My mother never slaps. The Samses' mother does. She does both those things. My mother pinches. It hurts but not as much as a spanking.

The Samses have to cut their own switches. "Mabel, you go out and get a switch and bring it in here," their momma will say. "You need a good whipping, and I'm going to give it to you." Her voice sounds like Brother Maypearl's on Sunday morning. Then I fly home, out the back door, by Mr. Mac's grocery store, down the alley, going fast where old man Taylor's working on his car. When one of the Samses is about to get a whipping, my feet never touch the ground.

My daddy's neck is my pillow. I put my nose in it and go to sleep. I open my eyes. It is beginning to get light. There is a thing in the room, big as a dragon. It does not move. I close my eyes. I open them. It is still there. My heart beats fast. I put my hand over it and hold it there so it will not thump its way out. I am scared. I am scared of this thing, and I am scared of my heart.

Mrs. House comes in. I lean across my pillow and point. "What's that?"

"A chair with your clothes on it."

"Who dressed it?"

She laughs, she hugs me, she picks me up. "You are a funny little girl, Miss Annie Ruth Lippincott. I dressed it. I put your clothes on it. Now you're going to be my little girl," she says, "until your mother's better."

Gingerbread. Hot gingerbread, out of the oven and into my mouth. Mother does not cut her gingerbread when it's hot, or her cake either. She puts them up. Sometimes she forgets them, and we have to throw them out.

I help Mrs. House. The grocery store and a penny of my own to spend. A sucker or a balloon. A bright red balloon. I choose the balloon. Taking the milk to Mr. Mac. The bread to Mr. Mac. When I knock on his back door, he smiles. "Good morning, Merry Sunshine," he says, like singing. Sometimes he gives me a nickel.

A box of animal cookies in my hand. The white string like a little suitcase handle. I like the lions with their big manes. I like the elephants and the giraffes. I eat them, first biting off their heads. I feel strong.

I run down the sidewalk. I stump my toe. I sit down and hold my foot up close with both hands so I can see my toe. Red blood is there. Waiting. Slowly it rises and overflows like milk in a glass. Suddenly, I want my mother. I cry. I cry louder and louder. Mrs. House comes out. She picks me up.

"I want, I, I, I want." I cannot finish because I am crying.

"Don't cry," she says. "Don't cry so hard. I know you want your mother. She'll be better soon and you can go home."

We rock. I suck my thumb. She smells like Ivory soap and cinnamon. I lay my head back. Her white, starched apron scratches my face. She sings:

Oh, don't you remember a long time ago
Two poor little babies
Their names I don't know.

I sleep. Days go by. Daddy comes for me. He is not the same. The frown stays on his forehead. It doesn't go away.

"I want to walk by myself," I say. I hold his hand and we walk to the car. I do not tell Mrs. House "good-bye." She is crying and I do not like for people to cry.

My mother cries when she is sick. But now she is well and she lies in bed. When I come in she holds out her arm to me. "Annie Ruth, I'm glad to see you."

I pretend not to see the arm waiting to hug me. I might let her hug me tomorrow. Every day people talk to her, people I cannot see and I cannot hear. I try. I tiptoe out on the porch and hide behind her rocking chair. She leans forward and holds tight to the arm of the chair. "Why don't you leave me alone? Go away." Her voice is loud. It scares me. "Why don't you leave me alone!" She takes off her shoe and throws it. "I said, 'Get away from me!'" I cannot take a breath now. Her voice is like cardboard tearing. Then she leans over on her knees and puts her arms around her head. She cries softly. "I haven't done anything to you," she says.

Mr. Mac walks by. He takes off his hat and nods. "Evening, Mrs. Lippincott," he says. Mother cannot see him when they are there. She cannot see me. They have yellow teeth and when they come in the night they eat corn. Mrs. House's chickens eat corn. Horses eat corn.

"Well, hello, Merry Sunshine," says Mr. Mac. I wriggle my fingers at him. He puts his hat back on and shakes his head back and forth as he walks on.

Mother sits up again. She sticks out her right hand. "You're mean! You'll be sorry you've said this to me," she says.

"Mother," I say. "Mother?" But she cannot hear me.

I run down to the pasture. I will build a house, a beautiful house. I will have the most beautiful house in the world. I stamp on the grass, and it is the floor. I squat down and bend the tall grass together over my head. Through it I can see the blue sky and the clouds like cotton balls. Never has there been such a roof. I crawl out and find a flat rock. I bring it in and put it in the middle of the house and it is the kitchen. I run back to the house, up on the porch past Mother in the rocking chair. She is leaning forward, holding her forehead with one hand. Her hair is yellow except at the top. There it is black.

In the kitchen I get a jar and fill it with water. Next I get some crackers. Then a spoon. I put the spoon in the jar and I hold the jar in one hand and the crackers in the other. I walk slowly back to my house. I try not to run.

I put the water and the crackers on the rock, and then I stamp out a bathroom. With a spoon, I dig a hole. It is the best part of a house. The bathroom. I pull down my panties to try out the bathroom. I think about a spider crawling out of the hole. A red ant. I cannot try out the bathroom. Tomorrow I will make a living room. I will pick some cotton blossoms and put them in a jar. It will be the most beautiful room in the whole world.

The sun is going down. Maybe Daddy is home. I run home. Mother is still on the porch. She is quiet. Daddy is not home. I get in bed. My sheets are gone but the pillow is there. I put my nose in my pillow and my thumb in my mouth. My toes wiggle down to the foot of the bed, safe and warm. I sleep.

I am going to school. Daddy and I walk to the grocery store. I get a new yellow box of Crayolas, a pencil, and a Big Chief writing tablet. The Crayolas are the best. I shiver as I think of the yellow suns, the green trees, and the red flowers I will color. The butterflies. The birds. I skip to school, holding Daddy's hand.

I love my school. Mrs. House's grown-up married daughter is my teacher. Miss Keenan. Her laugh is like Mrs. House's. The Samses are there. Two Samses in my room and Rory Lee Davis from down on the corner. Mother is sick. I walk from school to Mrs. House's. The Sams twins and Rory Lee walk behind me. They giggle. They sing:

Ha, ha, ha, ha, ha, ha,
Your momma's crazy
And your daddy's lazy.

I run. A pebble hits my leg. And another. Mrs. House comes out on the porch. "You get home!" She shakes her mop at them. "Trash! Nothing but trash! Now get on home! You ought to be ashamed of yourselves!"

She picks me up and we go inside and rock. She says, "Annie Ruth, you know what I'm going to do for my little girl?" I sit up straight in her lap. I shake my head. "Guess," she says.

"Cookies. You're going to make cookies?"

"Better! I'm going to make you a Shirley Temple dress!"

I catch my breath. Never have I thought I'd have a Shirley Temple dress. Not ever.

We go downtown to Smith's Dry Goods Store. Miss Margaret waits on us. She has red hair, and she smiles when she hears about the dress. She says, "Organdy?"

Mrs. House says, "Yes, organdy."

"Pink or blue?"

"Annie Ruth will decide."

I look at the pink. I think of cotton candy. I look at the blue. Like the sky. I choose the blue.

Then we get a pattern, whirls of blue ribbon, and thread.

"Tomorrow is Saturday. We'll make the dress," Mrs. House says. She tucks me in. On a chair by my bed she puts the blue organdy, the pattern, the ribbon, and the thread. I try to go to sleep in a hurry so morning will come. I think of the dress. I reach over and touch the ribbon, soft and shiny and blue. I go to sleep.

After breakfast, Mrs. House clears the table and wipes it off. "I'm going to cut out your dress," she says. "You run outside and play."

I go out and sit on the back steps. I can think of the dress.

I count to a hundred. Then I count again. Maybe the dress is done. I run around the house three times. I tiptoe inside. The dress is not finished.

"Annie Ruth. Child. All right you can stay if you're very quiet and very still. Now you can't say a word." Mrs. House's lips look like she's about to whistle. She frowns and she smiles. She talks to herself, not sounding one bit like my mother. "Trash," she says. "That's all they are. Heard it at home. Bound to."

She cuts and she bastes. Then she looks up and says, surprised. "Oh, Annie Ruth! There you are. Stand up in the chair, honey."

My nose itches but I do not scratch it. The dress is too pretty. My overalls come down and the dress drops over my head. It stands out all around. It is beautiful. It scratches my shoulders like Mrs. House's apron scratches my face when we rock.

"Stand still," she says. "I have to take your hem."

Where, I wonder.

Out of her mouth she takes a pin, then another, and another. Her mouth is filled with pins. I hope she does not swallow them.

"You can wear the dress to school on Monday," she says.

Mrs. House washes on Sunday. Nobody else washes on Sunday, but Mrs. House does when she has to. She does not go to church because she is on good terms with the Lord. "Lord knows, I'd like to go," she says, "but I've got too much to do." She washes in the back yard. When she finishes, she lets me bathe in the bluing water.

I wait while she boils the clothes. Then into a tub, through a wringer, into another tub and, finally, into the bluing water. The clothes in the blue water are beautiful. Some of the sheets stick up like snow-covered mountains. She pokes them with a stick. Down go the white mountains and up come others out of the clear blue water. I sit on the table and watch.

Finally, I get in the water. This is the ocean. Mrs. House washes my hair, my ears, my neck. She hands me the rag. "Wash down there," she says. She points between my legs.

Then she rolls up my hair. She puts her finger to my head and she brushes the hair around it. She does this over and over. She puts a bobby pin in each curl. She tucks me in. I cannot wait until morning. In the morning I cannot eat breakfast, but I drink my milk. Mrs. House says she is "journey proud" sometimes, and she cannot eat either.

Now! I hold my hands up and down comes my dress, floating down, tight around my waist with blue ribbons in a bow in back. My hair is in Shirley Temple curls. When I look in the mirror, I do not know myself. I am different. Like a butterfly. I am very pretty.

I am a queen when I walk into the schoolroom. Everyone whispers and looks at me. At recess the Samses say, "Let Annie Ruth choose. Annie Ruth, whose side do you want to be on?" I smile. They are my subjects. This is my due.

I wear my dress to school every day that week. When it gets cold, I wear it over my overalls. I wear it until the Samses come to school one day in pink Shirley Temple dresses. Then I put my dress on a shelf in my closet. Sometimes I take it out and look at it, but I never wear it again.

Olive

The sun comes through the stained glass window and falls on the two of them and upon the golden richness of the oaken casket. Olive stands looking straight ahead with an expression of cold indifference on her face. Her hands, however, are not indifferent. She grips the pew in front of her so that her knuckles are white, and the blue veins throb to the surface. She abruptly raises her hand and flicks it as if to brush away the intrusion of my gaze. As her hand settles back to curve over the top of the pew, Douglas puts his right hand over both of hers, holding them there, holding her there by his side. But he cannot hold her thoughts. No one knows what she thinks. John knew better than anyone.

If John had married me, perhaps I'd not be so struck down now by his death, and in 1962, when John's first wife died, everybody in Cold Springs thought he would. But I knew he wouldn't. I had always loved him, but someone once said, "We are elected into love," and I believe that. He just never loved me, just never came to it, and the next year I was less surprised than anyone when he came home with a bride. I woke up in the middle of the night, and when I looked through the pine trees to see lights on all through John's house, I felt a rush of joy just knowing he was home.

Early the next morning Amelia called. "John home yet?" she asked.

"Yes, he's home, but I haven't seen him. He's probably still asleep." The thought of John asleep, of his closeness, made me happy. I felt a stirring in my loins and smiled.

"Well, why don't you go over there and wake him up?" Amelia asked, reading my mind.

"And then what?" I said, but before she could answer I hung up, grinning foolishly and wishing I were young enough or confident enough to do that. As I looked out the window over my sink at John's car there in the drive, the early morning sun spilled away off the eaves so that my own face was reflected in the window, and I wondered how John saw my green eyes and wrinkled brow and mouth, encircled by almost invisible lines.

I lifted my chin and smiled at the window. "Oh, well," I told myself, "he's home, and we'll see each other before the sun sets today."

"Katherine, you ought to get out more," Amelia said frequently. "You're still pretty," this said hopefully, and then more positively, "*And* you're *very* funny."

But where does one go when one goes out, I wondered. In the fifties, although a widow did not climb upon the funeral pyre, she was psychologically shrouded so that her life often became a peripheral one, centered upon her coupled past. I, who had been in an uneven marriage for thirteen years would not choose to be in another. In those days divorce was as unusual as a happy marriage.

Still, I remember the repose of that splendid year before John married again—the long summer evenings overhung by pewtered skies, the smell of pines drummed into cold, crisp air by winter rains, the birdsong in the spring—four seasons enhanced by his comings and goings in his house next to mine.

Oh, he *must* have known I loved him the night Anna died, if he had allowed the knowing. He had called from the hospital, his voice so choked by grief, I hardly recognized him. "The doctor says Anna may die tonight," he said.

"I'll come right down," I told him, but when I got to the hospital, he was gone.

I stayed. I listened to the staccato sounds of the ticking clock (Invisible. Had I only imagined it?) and watched the sun dapple the gray-tiled floor. "Glory be to God for dappled things," I thought. "And glory be to Amelia's freckled nose and to her puppy's freckled coat. I picked up a newspaper and stared at the crossword puzzle. *A four letter word meaning place.* "H E R E." I furiously penciled it in. *You should be here, John. Not I.*

Sometime later a very young nurse came out. Her look swept around the room. "Where is Mr. Appleby?" she asked.

"I have no idea. I thought he was here."

"Mr. Appleby's been drinking," she said, her voice trembling.

"Judge Appleby's been suffering," I countered.

"Oh, is he a judge?" she asked, clearly incredulous. Then, "Well, I don't know about that, but Mrs. Appleby is dying. I think she is. And I'm the only nurse on duty right now." She hurried out of the room, but returned immediately. "She's gone!" she said, clearly astonished.

Thinking of John's disappearance, I said, "Gone? Gone where?"

She frowned. "I didn't know her. Not really. But I hope to a better place."

"You mean she died," I said. "If I see Judge Appleby I'll tell him," and picked up my purse and left.

I drove home in the darkness to two empty, cold houses. I had grieved for Anna these last months, and now I felt a mixture of sadness and relief. And astonishment. Death is always that, I thought.

I kicked off my shoes, took off my jacket, and called Amelia. "Poor thing," she said. "Two years is too long for anyone to suffer. How's John?"

"I haven't any idea. He wasn't with her when she died." When Amelia didn't respond, I said, "I suppose he's anesthetizing himself right now."

"I don't understand how a man could leave. . . ."

I interrupted her. "Neither do I," I said and hung up.

I cooked rice and chopped up baked chicken for soup. But when I poured it into a soup bowl, an apple looked tastier, and I picked one up and ate it. Then I finished the crossword puzzle I had begun in the hospital, put on a pair of tennis shoes and shorts and, in moonlight as bright as day, I jogged around the block. At 11:00 o'clock I showered, slipped on a gown and went through the house turning off lights and locking doors. Back in the kitchen again, a faint, plaintive "meow" reminded me I had not fed Cal. When I opened the screen door to feed him, I heard the squeak of the swing in his back yard.

"John," I called.

"Here, Katherine, I'm over here in the swing."

I slipped on my robe and padded barefooted over to his yard.

"Anna died," he said dully, mechanically.

"I know it. Why weren't you *there!*"

"No lectures, please. Just sit here with me." He patted the empty space beside him. "Sit down, Kate. I need to talk. To somebody," he added, slurring his words.

"John!" I cried. "Where *were* you?

He flinched, took a deep breath and sighed. "Oh, Lord," he said.

He said nothing more. From time to time he would start the swing, and we'd move back and forth for a minute, or he'd reach over the side and pick up his glass and drink from it before carefully setting it down.

When he began to talk, his speech was clear but filled with anger. "Anna," he said, "Anna was never happy. To live and never be happy is to never be whole. Remember that poem you read to us? Last summer? Those lines from Eliot? 'I have heard the mermaids singing; I do not think that they will sing to me.' And Anna had. She had heard them. She knew she was missing the fullness of life but . . . . Kate, do you know how sad that is? Better, better not to hear them."

All that he said was true. "But there were times when she seemed—" I began.

"Seemed! Seemed!" He turned in the swing and looked at

me. "Katherine, you're happy. What makes you happy? Your silly roses? Your silly cat? Your silly . . . . Katherine, did your husband make you happy?"

I laughed, startled into honesty. "My silly husband? Well he never made me unhappy."

"Kate, oh, Kate," he said, picking up his glass. "Happiness is a gift."

"John, you've been happy," I insisted. "Not now, not since Anna's illness. Before that. You enjoyed your practice and your books and your friends."

He smiled. "And dancing. Don't forget dancing! But I never made Anna happy." His voice was filled with wonder and regret. "I never made her happy." Now his voice went flat, devoid of energy. "After a while, I stopped trying."

John's love of poetry had always beguiled me. When he took my hand and kissed it, my anger melted away.

I had not noticed the fine mist that had begun to fall until I put my hand on the arm of the swing and felt its wetness. "John, come in. I made some soup."

"No, no soup today. But I'll walk you home."

Arm in arm we walked across his property and through the garden gate. When we started up my kitchen steps, John stumbled and I turned and brushed his face, and he was in my arms and I in his, and nothing, not Anna's death, not old voices, not God himself could have stilled the passion that swept us from the porch to my bed that night. He, made so by Anna's long illness, was as starved as I and, afterwards, I felt at ease lying there in his arms. Then the words gathered: "John, I've always . . . ." But "God!" he said and was asleep.

In the morning, he was gone. I went to Anna's funeral,

but it was a month before I saw him again. When I answered the light knock on my back door, he stood there, arms folded across his chest, frowning. "Katherine, the thing that happened the night Anna died. I'm sorry."

Oh, terrible words to describe the passion we gladly shared that night. I did not know how to answer words like "thing," and "sorry." I turned away, turned back. "John," I said. "Let's just forget it. Don't look so sad. We are what we've always been. Just good friends. What happened just happened. It's over."

"Oh, well now," he said. "That's good. Katherine, you're a . . . ."

"Go," I said. "Just go." He kissed my check and was gone.

That last year John had become my closest friend, besides Amelia. We depended on each other.

Startled when the phone began to ring again, "It's Amelia," I told myself. "She's calling again about John." But it was John's voice I heard when I answered the phone.

"Katherine, come over here. I have a surprise for you."

"Give me a minute," I said.

He's brought me a present, I thought. Glancing at his mail stacked on the settle bench in my bedroom, I splashed cold water on my face, brushed my teeth and then my hair, stepped into gray slacks and slipped on a blue silk blouse, hurrying, hurrying because I couldn't wait to see him.

When I stepped into his kitchen, I saw a young girl perched on the edge of the kitchen table. She gazed at me and smiled.

"John talks about you a lot. Nothing that you wouldn't be proud to hear," she added.

How vividly moments of shock etch details into one's mind! The scene is as fixed as if it were before my eyes. I remember the softly moving, patterned dance on the yellow pine floor created by the sun's coming though the Swiss-embroidered curtains when I took Olive's hand. I remember her carelessly buttoned blouse, her sleepy eyes and rumpled hair. She, Olive, was almost slatternly looking and would have been completely so had it not been for her youth. Because of this there was a childlike innocence in her slender body as she moved lightly around the kitchen. When I sat down at the wide-planked oak table across from John, and Olive poured coffee, I noticed, and resented (moments of pettiness for expiation) that she had set the table with Anna's sterling silver and Meissen china.

At that moment, my kitten's plaintive meow signaled he was at John's kitchen door. Olive opened the screen door for him. "Kitty, kitty," she purred. "Come in. No need to be cranky. Here, here's a little milk," she cooed, pouring the milk into one of Anna's fine saucers. When she set it on the floor, I looked at John and saw that he was smiling fatuously at her.

"Olive was the receptionist at the O'Shea firm in North Carolina," he said. "I asked her out to lunch ten minutes after I walked into the office."

Then I, obtusely, stupidly, "Olive, how long will you be here in Cold Springs?"

John threw back his head and laughed, "Katherine, Katherine, we're married. Olive and I were married a week ago in Salem."

"Oh, God," I cried, but not aloud, then woodenly, "I hope you'll be happy."

The lameness of my response brought John's head up sharply so that he hesitated, but then he began again, and was soon carried away by his account of their courtship. I could not look at him. I wanted to spare him the embarrassment he must feel because of her revealing blouse and dialect and because she was barely twenty-one and he was fifty-one and, by then, a federal judge. But John seemed almost giddy as he told me he had proposed to Olive the first time he'd had dinner with her and that she had accepted the third time. Olive listened, not saying anything, but she never took her eyes off John.

"Olive loves cats and gardening. You two will be great friends," John was saying eagerly.

"I'm sure we will," I said. "I'll call you, Olive, one day soon."

I went home feeling old and abandoned, and determined to forget all about John and his silly marriage, but I reckoned without Olive.

Olive's skin *was* quite dark and by the next day it was all over town that John had picked her right out of a cotton patch. Her hair was black and hung straight to her shoulders. On Saturday when I stopped for gas, old Mr. Taylor asked me how I liked living next door to a good-looking dish like that. He said, "Them Indians, they're good-lookin'!" Can Indians be blue-eyed, I wondered?

In a week the town had decided to crucify her because of old loyalties to Anna and even, I suppose, to me. Without money or family or education, she was simply too young and pretty. Mrs. Briggs called to say she had heard that Olive's father was a wrestler called Tokyo Joe. Virginia Osbourne asked if I'd noticed how she butchered the King's English. (I had.) Amelia called and said, "Now, Katherine, you know I don't care who her father is or how she talks, but I'll tell you one thing! That marriage will never work! There's just not enough *there*. It won't last three months."

I said, "Well, who knows?" but I thought she was right.

I could easily ignore John's foolishness. He was up early and gone all day, but Olive was a constant presence. Each morning she worked in her garden, and I worked in mine. We each knew how to make things grow, but we went at it differently. I fertilized, sprayed, weeded, watered, pruned, and clipped. She watered a little and weeded some, but mostly she just seemed to enjoy her flowers. She'd reach out and cup with her hands the biggest of the Peace roses growing there by the fence. When she leaned over to smell the rose, it was as if all her being was centered there on those soft, delicate petals. Her rose beds were not edged or fertilized, but her roses were full and sweet smelling. If she knew she was being snubbed by the town and by me, she didn't seem to care.

One April morning, I was troweling my rose bed, working in a little fertilizer, and hoping the darkening cumulous clouds would gather enough moisture for a summer rain. Cal was on the picnic table playing with his tail. When he backed himself off the edge, he landed on his four feet, looked around as if embarrassed, and disappeared around the corner of the house. I chuckled, and Olive burst out laughing. When our eyes met, I said, "Let's stop a minute for a glass of iced tea."

Over the summer, I became Olive's friend because I enjoyed her. Her laughter was contagious. She could mimic anyone. The mailman: "Good mownin' Miss Olive. Got some mail for you. Right here in my good right hand," she would drawl, making three syllable words out of one. And Amelia: "My dear.

You have a little magic in your gardening. Would you tell me your secrets," she'd say in perfect imitation of Amelia's faintly British Tennessee accent. And she was so grammatically quick that I enjoyed teaching her. If she said, "It don't" and I came right after and said, "It doesn't" that's all she needed. When she and John began to entertain, I taught her how to set a table and when to offer wine or bring in coffee. "Three forks," she giggled once, when we were setting the table in John's dining room. "Let's leave one off! See if anyone notices. And if they notice, will they say anything?" And with her twinkling eyes and infectious laughter, I couldn't have kept from laughing if I had tried.

When John's work slowed, the three of us would sometimes sit out in the back yard having a drink on a summer's night and John, talking about this or that trial, would as often begin the telling with "Katherine" as with "Olive." I enjoyed hearing him say my name.

"Katherine Hopkins, you're way beyond *silly*," I'd lecture myself. But I couldn't keep from loving John anymore than I could keep my heart from beating.

Once he thanked me. "Katherine, you've been good to me and to Olive. We won't forget it ever!" And, that had to be enough.

Olive and John had been married sixteen years when John had his stroke. I thought I was dreaming when I heard Olive calling, "Katherine, Katherine. Come quick. Oh, dear God. Hurry!"

The minute I saw him I knew. I called the ambulance and stood by his bed, hearing the terrible, labored sound of his breathing. "John, John, John," I said over and over again like a litany.

"John, can you hear me?" Olive asked. He lifted his left arm about a foot in the air. She cradled his head in her arms. "Oh, John. Help is on the way. Oh, my love, my darling."

At first there was hope. "In the morning we'll run some tests. We'll know more then," the doctor said. But after the tests he said, "Time. Only time will tell how much the judge will recover."

John lived. But at times I longed for his death. Once I saw an eagle in a small cage. Imprisoned, it sat on the floor, not even on a bar, and in its eyes was a look of fierce rage. John's eyes looked like that those first few weeks. After a month he came home from the hospital, diminished. Diminished in every way. Once so magnificently alive, he was now a gravely serious, sweetly quiet, old man. Words came slowly to him or not at all, and most of the time he merely listened, or perhaps, only seemed to listen.

Olive and I took turns with the nursing. We fed him, we bathed him, and we changed his clothes for he was incontinent. I grew impatient and tired and bored, not with John, but with his illness. However, Olive never did. Now it was her face that came alive when she went into his room.

"Oh, Katherine," she said, "at least he's alive!" And she meant it. On any terms, she'd keep him.

"Most of his recovery will be made these first three months," the doctor said. "He's a strong man, and he will live, but I can't tell you now how complete his recovery will be. I just do not know."

John soon learned to compensate for his paralyzed left side

so that propped up with pillows he could sit fairly comfortably in his wheelchair. But helping him to bed at night took two strong people. After working with John one afternoon, the therapist shook her head.

"I just don't know," she said. "I'm not sure Judge Appleby's trying."

"Katherine, we'll have to help him more. We'll have to work harder," Olive said firmly. Her buoyancy kept us afloat those first few months.

Every town needs a saint and now Cold Springs had one. "She's the sweetest thing to him," old man Taylor said. And visiting John was not depressing. When Olive leaned to rearrange John's pillows or showed him a perfect rose from the garden or just sat close to him, his eyes would brighten and his little crooked smile would appear. Then we could all smile—at John, at Olive, at each other. Olive kept a sideboard replenished with tea or bourbon, and her chatter, as she arranged a vase of flowers or mimicked a young lawyer's flat, South Texas accent, was cheerful.

Thus, dulled by the sameness of the routine upon which an invalid's life must be centered, we lived through those first weeks. And then Douglas Adair moved in, exploding the bubble of listlessness in which the three of us had become enveloped.

Doug had been a casual friend of Olive's and John's for years. The first time I had met him was at their home, hers and John's. They were celebrating their tenth Christmas together with a party. Entertaining. During their annual Christmas party, with the Christmas tree trimmed and decorated and candles burning and the smell of pine filling the house, Doug, not long out of law school and the newest member of John's firm, was talking to John and me, but John was not listening, and I knew he was waiting for Olive. His eyes moved restlessly around the room, and then she came into the room and John relaxed. She was wearing a black velvet dress and John's Christmas pearls that glistened on her dark neck and on the lighter shade of the upward swell of her breasts. When she came in, the whole room brightened. Olive moved from one group to another, leaning forward intently, listening, until she reached John's side. As they talked to me and to Douglas, it was as if they had always been together. He leaned his head forward to listen to her and, in spite of the difference in their ages, there was no mistaking their love for each other.

I left the party early and went home and thought about Olive and John and, for some reason, about Doug too. An ambitious young man, I thought, but nice. Over the next years he was in and out of their house, through his marriage that lasted a year and his separation and divorce that lasted three. He would stop by after tennis or on his way to the lake, and John soon became the young lawyer's mentor. "Doug's coming along," he would say, pleased. Or, once, "I wish you could have heard the paper he presented about the ethics of business law. As good as I've ever heard."

Among Texas men, Doug was an anomaly. Looking like a derrick man in his blue jeans and worn boots, he moved with authority in the masculine world of guns and boats and county politics. Yet, he was equally at home in the company of women, enjoying the talk of good food, admiring a fine piece of needlepoint, or discovering a new rose in Olive's garden. He merited John's highest praise: "Doug has integrity." For me,

Doug had a kind of innocence, a disarming honesty, much like Olive's own.

After John's stroke, Doug became the main link to his law office, and his visits assumed a regular pattern. On Wednesdays and Fridays we counted on him to help entertain John, pulling and tugging wisps of smiles or labored phrases from him in much the same way that we had pulled and tugged his body (how heavy paralysis had made it!) from place to place. The best times for all of us came when Doug would bring along his guitar, and then the evenings recovered their old tenderness, as bound together by the past and the music, we could live again.

One Wednesday afternoon an unseasonable cool spell blew into Cold Springs from West Texas. The dust in the air, the force of the wind, and the trees swaying heavily against the hazy sky, made the world feel hard. I longed to stay home with a good book, but, instead, I threw my sweater over my shoulders and ran over to John's house right after supper. That evening even Olive seemed out of sorts, most likely dulled by the weather. We watched Doug lay a fire and then we sat silently as the flames flickered and caught.

"How about some Irish folk tunes?" Doug said speaking into the fire amid the silence. We looked expectantly at John, and my heart turned over at the sweetness of his smile. Words still came to John with great difficulty, and now he merely nodded his pleasure at the idea.

Doug tuned his guitar and when he began to sing, John kept time with his left forefinger and once he hummed along. In the firelight Olive's cheeks were the color of raspberries, and her blue eyes, reflecting the bank of hot coals, looked almost black. When Doug played the tune called "A Bunch of Wild Thyme," that begins *Come all you maidens fair,* and ends with *Let no man steal away your thyme,* Olive quickly moved over behind John's chair, put her arms around him and kissed him, laughing.

"Oh, Johnny. We'll soon be dancing to those songs. I know we will."

John did not respond, did not so much as squeeze her hand. Abruptly, Doug put down his guitar and stood up. "John," he said, "if you're about ready, we'll get you to bed, and then I'll take off. I'm going to Mexico City tomorrow."

Olive walked us to the door. She leaned forward and kissed me, then Doug. "Thank you for the music. It does us all good."

Can one grow accustomed to any idea, I wonder? I suppose I had known for weeks that Olive and Doug had begun to see each other, and even, if I had thought about it, that they had become lovers. But John's recovery was so painfully slow that I did not think about Olive much at all.

One morning in June, Olive called. "Katherine, Doug has to drive out to the old Lawson place on the Summerhill road, and I'm going to ride out with him. Mrs. Stanley's here with John, but if you'd like a game of Patience, come over. You'd be most welcome."

We had almost finished the game when they came in. I heard Doug's voice, the words indistinguishable, followed by Olive's bell-like laughter. She's not laughed like that in a long while, I thought, and I was glad she had had a good time.

"Doug's been offered a partnership with a firm in San

Francisco," she told me after John was asleep. "He's considering it. Katherine, think about living there. In one of the most
beautiful cities of the world! How can he refuse?" But a week
later, as Olive and Doug helped John into bed, Doug's fingers
curled over the tips of Olive's, and Doug's San Francisco offer
was not mentioned again.

The night Doug told Olive she had to leave John and marry
him, she was sadder than I'd ever seen her. I'd gone out to
plant some King Alfred jonquils to replace those the plumb-
ers had killed when they laid the new sewer line to the street.
Once that was done I'd worked a while longer pulling weeds.
The two had strolled casually toward the fence between our
properties, I thought, to speak to me, when suddenly he put his
hands on her shoulders and shook her. "Goddamnit," he said.
"I want you at the head of my table and I want you in my bed.
John's had a full life, a good life, but you, Olive. What about
you? Sitting across from an old man, night after night. What
do you have together? What do you share? Any nurse could do
the things you do for him. Olive, he's sick; if he were his old self
he would tell you to go!"

"Stop it, Douglas! Stop it!" she said.

Doug was silent for a minute. Then he came at the subject
again but from a different angle, "Olive, you've always wanted
a child, and we could have the most beautiful children. We
can't wait forever. You're shackled to a man who's slowly dying,
but I don't intend to stop living because of John. He's stealing away our time." Doug started to his car, stopped, turned
around, and came back. "I'm going to Mexico City next week,"
he said. "If you change your mind, call me. I'll be at the Del

Prado." Now he looked at me. "Sorry, Katherine. Maybe you can talk some sense into her."

Olive stood there for a long time after he drove away. Then she shrugged her shoulders and went inside without a word. But I was sure I knew what her answer would be.

Three days after Doug had flown to Mexico City, I was painting a chair when Olive wandered over and picked up a brush to help. Then I fixed iced tea for us and we sat in their swing to drink it. When Cal ran by chasing an invisible insect, Olive put her glass down, grabbed him, and sat back in the swing, cradling him in her arms.

"Katherine, I'm going out of town for a few days. The nurse will be here and the sitters, of course, but would you see that John's properly taken care of?"

As she looked down at Cal, rubbing his stomach, her black hair fell forward so that I could not see her face. But the memory of the anguish in Doug's voice came flooding back so that my response was kinder then it might have been: "Of course, I'll see about John."

I thought she had decided to meet Doug in Mexico and take up their past again. I didn't like it but by then my life was such a part of theirs, I couldn't refuse. When Olive kissed John goodbye and turned to pick up her bag, tears ran down her face, the only tears I ever saw Olive shed.

She came back ten days later, and soon Floyd Tubb was walking through the old carriage house out back, sketching and nodding and measuring. The decaying wooded floors were torn away and the bricks underneath were scrubbed and waxed. The walls were plastered and whitewashed except for the almost black crossbeams, and the porch was extended so that the wicker furniture fit comfortably on it. A small kitchen and hospital-like bath were added. Olive did not explain the remodeling, and I just assumed she needed to put more distance between herself and John's invalidism.

The day after the workers finished, Olive moved John into the carriage house, and then, over a glass of wine, she told me she had gotten a Mexican divorce and married Doug.

I was furious. I had never touched anyone in anger, but I wanted to slap her. "I don't believe you," I said. "I'm not going to listen to this!" I shouted, backing away from her. "How could you? How could you do this to John?"

Olive looked at me, steadily. "It is what it is," she said softly.

"What in heaven's name does *that* mean!" I cried, aware of the blue jays in the garden calling angrily at the cat. When she did not answer, I stormed out.

I did not sleep that night. When the sun came up I drove over to Amelia's. When I told her, sobbing, what Olive had done, she was satisfyingly furious. "He should have married you," she said. "But now I'm glad he didn't. He was a fool to marry that little nobody. Katherine, times have changed. You'll meet some nice man. You could travel together. This day and age, Cold Springs wouldn't think a thing about it."

I had to laugh. Amelia's dream had always been that I would meet another man (almost any would do), fall in love, get married, and live happily. But now she seemed to be suggesting a lover. Still laughing, I said, "Oh, Amelia, you just never give up. And you're wrong about John and Olive. John worships her. Olive loves him."

"When he was healthy," she said scornfully.

"Amelia, I wish I hadn't come. Please don't tell anyone about this. You know how Cold Springs is."

"What's said in this kitchen, stays in this kitchen," Amelia said firmly. And I knew that was true.

Refreshed by Amelia's staunch friendship, I drove home, put the car in the garage, and walked around back just as Olive rolled John out onto the porch of the carriage house and went inside. John's eyes caught mine. He looked ashamed of his illness, of Olive's behavior, of a world which had become for him an embarrassingly miserable place in which to live. I walked over and knelt by his chair, took his hand and held it to my face. "John," I said.

With his good right arm he held my head to his side for a long moment. I looked up into his face and saw he was struggling to speak, his mouth moving soundlessly until, finally, "Ah . . . , ah . . . " And then he sighed, a long, shuddering sigh.

"Olive," I said.

He nodded, and his eyes looked out across the roof of my house, across the tops of the trees. Not even his fragility could mask the sorrow that he felt. And so we began again, the three of us.

Over the next weeks I came to understand that the evenings and nights belonged to Douglas and the mornings and the days to John as far as Olive was concerned. And in a few months, I could chuckle to myself over the idea that John had the best of it from both of us. Olive would spend the day with John and his friends and then about the time the sun was going down, Mrs. Stanley would come for the evening and night, and Olive would go inside to be there when Doug came home.

Before Doug's car pulled out of the driveway the next morning, Olive was out at the carriage house walking lightly across
the porch with the morning paper in her hands. While the bacon fried, she helped John with his morning routine, and then
she'd make the toast and scramble the eggs. After breakfast
she would sit close to John, reading to him the news from the
paper she knew would interest him. Old man Taylor told me
one day that, "No sirree, a daughter couldn't be no better than
Olive is to John. It don't matter what nobody says." In a few
months, to all of us, Olive became the child John had never
had, and we ceased to wonder at this sad miracle.

The old carriage house became my favorite place to be.
Red begonias trailed down the hanging baskets, and the bright
green and white cushions on the teak furniture made the clean,
white porch look like spring. The magazines and the newest
books piled carelessly about, the bowl of fruit on the table,
and the schnauzer puppy Olive had given John made everyone
welcome. On Christmas day Olive had come out barefooted
in her jeans with Posh, her Christmas present for John. "He
needs something that doesn't feel sorry for him," she told me.
Standing there, except for the grey in her hair, she looked very
much as she had looked that first day in her kitchen so many
years earlier.

At first, John's friends and neighbors came because they
felt so bad over what Olive had done to him. And some came
because they were curious to see the principals of this unlikely
drama. Then, no longer either pitying or curious, they came
because visiting John and Olive was . . . *reassuring*.

As for Doug he might as well have been on another planet.
During all those months I never heard Olive say a word about

him, and, so far as I knew, he never even stepped upon the porch of the carriage house.

All this lasted until the day before yesterday when John didn't wake up from his nap. Olive and Doug will be free to leave Cold Springs now. They will most likely move to a bigger city, a larger firm, although she'll always come back to see me. Married to the only man I ever loved, she's come to be the daughter I never had. I'll miss her. The town will too. Chuckling, Amelia said, "When Olive leaves, whatever will we find to talk about?"

Spurs That Jangle

There was a darkness of energy, an undefined relentlessness of will about our new neighbor. His walk for one thing. His heels coming down hard so that when he walked across the lawn his boots dug in, tearing out tender little sprigs of grass. And the dark flamboyance of his dress: the heavy, black leather gloves and vest that belied the gentleness of his blue eyes and the sweetness of his slightly lopsided smile. But Linda, my sister, never noticed these anomalies, and from the first her attitude toward him was one of fatuous sponsorship.

Linda saw our new neighbor first that hot summer Sunday. As was our custom, we had walked to church, to Bryce's for lunch, and then home.

"Well, Ella, you've wanted children in the neighborhood. They've come," she said.

Relieved at her matter-of-fact tone, my eyes followed the line of her gaze, and I saw that the driveway next to ours was filled with a confusion of sound and color. A bare-chested, slender, blond-headed man unloaded a red pickup, effortlessly plucking a playpen and a highchair from the top of the furniture-jumbled pile. Before we reached the walkway, he had taken these inside and returned with another man, also shirtless, but with a heavy, black beard, and together they carried in a rolling, rollicking mattress that seemed to have a life of its own. A young girl, barefooted, wearing shorts, watched the unloading. On her right hip, thrust forward, she held a baby, bracing it with her arm.

Only that morning (and this with increasing frequency), Linda had said, "Ella, our neighborhood's changing." She mourned each change. When the Tilson house was torn down, her silence hummed with anger and, shortly afterwards, the old Victorian next to it was razed, and she spoke wistfully of buying both lots but we, of course, had not the resources. The McLarty house next door had only recently been turned into a beehive of apartments, and it was into one of these that the furniture was disappearing that Sunday morning.

I went up our walk and into the house, surprised when Linda did not immediately follow. She had walked across our lawn and was talking with the young men and the girl. When she came in she was smiling and she hummed a song I'd not heard since I was a young girl. "I've got spurs that jingle, jangle, jingle," she hummed, and the words sprang into my mind: *As I go riding merrily along.*

That evening as we sat in the kitchen eating our early Sunday supper of corn flakes and fruit, we heard a knock on the door, a sound so light I would have believed it to be imagined had Linda not looked across at me, eyebrows raised.

"I'll go," I said, pushing my chair back. Our new neighbor stood on the back steps.

"Hi," he said and smiled, the blue of his eyes almost hidden by the cat-like, elliptical-shaped pupils.

"Yes?" I said, quickly adding, "You're the new neighbor."

"I met your sister. She tell you? Well, I'm Mark. We're getting settled," he added grinning, "It's just Lupe and me. And old Matt. Ridin' herd on us all."

Mark stood, leaning against the doorframe, his thumbs tucked into the waistband of his hip-hugging jeans; his blue eyes, however, probed our kitchen, focused on Linda, seated at the kitchen table. My throat felt tight. I didn't like him, and he knew it. When he looked at me, he quickly stepped back, away from the door.

I tried to smile. "It's been a long time since we've had children in the neighborhood. My sister and I have missed them," I said truthfully.

"It's about Matt I've come. We forgot to get milk. Could we borrow some until tomorrow?" Smiling, he opened the door and stepped inside so that now I was the one who retreated.

"Oh, of course." I turned to get the milk, but Linda was already there, smiling and handing him a full, half-gallon carton.

"Here, take this. We've got plenty," she said.

We both knew this was all we had and that we would not be grocery shopping until Tuesday. I am the one, not Linda, who is usually free with the giving. My sister believes that were it not for her, we'd soon be in the poorhouse. "And then who will take care of us?" she reminds me.

Although I have lived with my sister our whole lives long except for the twelve days she was married, I do not know her well, am never sure of her responses. Between Linda and me there lies a comfortable space wedged apart by bits and pieces of times unshared.

The milk was not returned the next day, but Linda did not notice. The next evening the light knock came again and Linda answered the door. After a while she returned smiling radiantly. "Mark's going to mow our lawn, Ella, in exchange for guitar lessons. He's interested in learning gospel music."

"You haven't touched a guitar in years," I said. "Linda, this is foolish."

She giggled. "Oh, Ella, some things you just don't forget," she said, pushing her hair to the top of her head.

The lessons began the next day. Lupe, with Matthew straddling her hip, came along with Mark, who had a battered old guitar slung over his shoulder. When Linda began the fine old hymn, "Amazing Grace," Mark grinned and his long, sinuous fingers moved carefully over the strings, mocking the piano's full-bodied tone, upstaging its rhythm, clouding the melody.

I was astonished by Linda's response. My sister, who can play Chopin without one hint of false sentiment, laughingly joined Mark's treatment with tremolos, interpolations, and retards. I looked away and saw Lupe's bare feet, her obviously braless breasts beneath her tee shirt. I saw the ugly sores on the fretful baby's arm and went into the kitchen to get the camphophenique. When I began to dab this on the sores, Matthew's fretfulness became a loud wail.

Hearing Linda's solicitous, "Oh, Ella. You've hurt Matthew," I slipped outside to cut some daisies for the breakfast table.

During the days that followed, the disorder of our neighbor's lives crept over into ours like a parasitic disease. Food was borrowed and not returned; harsh, cacophonous music disturbed our sleep; and the motorcycles and trucks, parked continuously across our sidewalk, became permanent fixtures so that we, unthinkingly, walked around them as we had always walked round the sharp abutments in the sidewalk. Like a flock of birds, the young moved always with others; energetically eating, talking, repairing motorcycles; or they swirled noisily off for a few days so that the house next door was emptily, ominously silent. Matthew, singularly unappealing to me, looked silently out at his world from a papoose-like contraption strapped to Lupe's back or sitting on a frayed, slightly dirty, yellow blanket. Always with the young, he never seemed to sleep but sat gazing about unblinkingly, as if retreating like some old man from the discordant energy in which he lived.

Last Saturday Mark came to mow the lawn. "Miss Ella, when I mow your lawn, could I just roll the mower right over and do mine? We're having a party tonight."

I felt a mild surge of resentment at his address, the former implying respect and the latter familiarity, neither of which I believe he felt. A newly-discovered self wanted to say, "Return the milk first," or "That is not our agreement." I did not like this part of my nature so I ignored it, but I did not return Mark's smile.

"Come out to the garage," I told him. "I'll show you where it's kept."

The tin-roofed garage was the only part of our lives, perhaps the only part of Cold Springs, that had remained unchanged. Its dirt floor was packed so hard that the faint odor of oil was constant and strangely comforting. To the right hung my father's tools; some hanging there belonged to his father before him. Gleaming like new and hanging high on the walls were my grandmother's number two washtubs, shiny and galvanized so that when the door was open and the light came in, the garage sprang to life.

"Wow," Mark said. "This is really neat!" Like a gentle but predatory cat's, his eyes moved over the pliers, the screwdrivers, and the nails, separated according to size in plastic boxes on the shelves. A brace, saws, and hammers were all arranged neatly along the right side of the garage.

"Who keeps it for you?"

"Nobody keeps it. We don't use it much. Here's the mower, the oil, and the sharpener."

The hand mower was small, perfect for our yard.

"Ella," Linda called, and I answered as Mark rolled the mower out.

Linda beamed, "Mark, how nice! Getting right to the lawn!" She was fatuous as she stood watching him push the lawn mower away, his boot heels cutting sharp, little rectangular tracks in the lush summer grass.

I was comforted by the orderliness of the garage. I fully understand my ancestor's reverence for order, their belief in it. "One can take comfort in things in right places," I told myself, and felt the tension slip away.

"Silly," I told myself. "Linda's right. Young people keep one young."

"Broken!" I heard her say later that evening. "Oh Mark, that's too bad. Ella, the old mower's broken. Well, it was worn out anyway." Her voice was warm. "Just don't you worry about it."

The harsh staccato sounds of Mark's boots became fainter and fainter as he retreated to his apartment. "He's mowed his yard and one-third of ours," I said sharply, retrieving the oil can from the sidewalk and the sharpener from the rose bed. "He ruined it. It can't be fixed."

"Oh, Ella, don't be silly! It's just an old mower."

Tone, scent, sound, catching one unawares, tearing away the years, tumbling them off so they fall away and the unbidden appears. The wound is opened. Suddenly I am twelve years old again and Linda is saying, "Oh, Mother, don't be silly."

Mother does not want Linda to be married on Christmas day. It's cold outside and I blow my breath on the windowpane, playing tic-tac-toe, enjoying the coolness of the moisture on my forefinger.

"I do know him, and he's going off to war. He may be killed," Linda cries out.

"He may not be," Mother says grimly. "And you don't know him."

"Mama, I am going to marry Jack on Christmas Day."

"We'll see what your father says about that," Mother says.

Linda runs crying from the room and up the steps. Her door slams. I look at Mama.

"Mama, I like Jack," I said, and I did. I liked the way he bounded up on the porch, his boot heels coming down hard on the steps, announcing his arrival before his knock on the door. I liked the way he always stopped when he saw me, put his hands on my shoulders, planted a kiss on my forehead and asked, "How's my very prettiest girl?"

Jack had been in town only a week, but a week seeing him every day was to me a month, a year, an infinite time. In those seven days, he had taught me all the words and we'd sing together while Linda accompanied us on her ukulele:

I got spurs that jingle, jangle, jingle,
As I go riding merrily along.
And they sing, 'oh, ain't you glad you're single?'
And the song ain't so very far from wrong.

But all the time we sang, he never took his eyes off Linda. Swinging lazily back and forth in the porch swing, he watched her like a cat ready to pounce.

The next day, Linda was gone. Mother found the note, dressed, and went downtown to tell Papa. Silence filled our house. We put up a Christmas tree, baked cookies and cake, and wrapped packages; but the sounds, the smells—the *joy*—of Christmas was gone as if Linda had packed it up and taken it away, along with her new blue dress and white cotton gown.

Throughout those long twelve days, Daddy sat smoking his pipe on the front porch, his face turned always toward the highway over which Linda must have gone. Mother worked silently, without stopping: dusting, polishing, cooking, from early in the morning until sundown, neither of them giving a thought to me.

Two days after Christmas she came home. I opened the door and found her there on the porch, looking down at the swing that swayed with the breeze. She was pale, unaware of my presence, hypnotized by the slow movement of the empty swing.

"Linda, Linda! We've missed you!" I hugged her hard.

She patted my shoulder. "I'm glad," she said, but she wasn't. I had never seen anyone look so sad.

"You'll have to talk to Papa," Mother told her, and that evening Papa climbed the steps to her room. After a long time he came down.

"Our girl's come home to stay," was all he said, and he went out and sat on the porch swing. He was there when we went to bed and there when I got up the next morning.

"Aren't you glad she's home?" I asked Mother.

"Oh, Ella, yes. But honey, I wish I'd been wrong about Jack. This time I wish I had been wrong."

Then she put her cuptowel over her face and cried. I put my arms around her and cried too, not knowing why.

Now I looked at Linda, remembering the pain she'd caused so long ago.

"Matthew's always wet, and he cries all the time," I said cruelly.

Linda whirled around and went outside. She worked in her rose garden all afternoon, not even stopping for a nap.

That evening their party swirled around us. Young people came on motorcycles, in pick-up trucks, and in cars. Blankets were spread, beer cans popped open, and the music rose and fell and rose again. The McLarty's back screen door was opened and closed with annoying irregularity. Linda sat by her up- stairs window, savoring each detail. She might have been ob- serving the tuning up of a great symphonic orchestra.

"They're building a fire," she said. Then, "Oh, now Mark's playing the guitar," and her smile as she gazed out the window was beneficent.

Uneasy, I felt drawn again and again to join in her con- stant attendance at the window. The music grew louder. Mark was cooking on a raised brick grill over an open fire. Into a big washtub, he emptied sacks of vegetables. Soon I smelled the odor of onions and garlic. Three or four young people helped him cook, while others sprawled on blankets or leaned against motorcycles. Matthew, propped up with pillows, lay on a blanket and I could not tell if he was fretful. The careless young filled the McLarty's back yard, spilling over into ours.

The smell of grilled fish reminded me of my own hunger. "Linda, I'm going to eat supper," I said. "Would you like something other than cereal?"

"I think a little toast would be nice, and some tea," she said.

She came downstairs with me and over supper my spirits rose. A party in the neighborhood was a change after all. We put the dishes away, folded and hung the linen dish towels, and swept up the floor.

Linda went upstairs to resume her greedy vigil. I tried to read and, failing, walked out into the pewtered evening with its musky scent of magnolias and honeysuckle drummed into the air by the loud rock music. I walked a long way, away from the harsh, rhythmic sounds of the party next door, and as I walked images of Jack, Linda's old love, and Mark met, overlapped, merged and the song came floating back:

And they sing, 'Oh ain't you glad you're single?'
And the song ain't so very far from wrong.

And underlying the carefree words, the rhythm I now heard was harsh and heavy, more a part of this hot muggy night than of that sad sweet time so long ago.

I walked until I was very, very tired and then, somewhat eased, I went home and to bed, uncaring whether Linda slept or not. In the night, and I do not know how long I had slept, the motorcycles exploded into life. Startled, I sat up in bed and Linda was suddenly there beside me. Once, twice, three times they raced around our house, through our garden, across the front lawn and onto the sidewalk again.

"I'm going to call the police," I said, leaving Linda sitting heavily on my bed. By the gas lights of the water company shining into our backyard, I could see the heavy ruts, the rose bushes torn and shattered, and the washtub, and now I recognized it, the once brightly shining washtub, blackened and bent, abandoned over the still-burning red coals of the fire. At that moment the police arrived and the young people scattered. An officer led Mark, swaying slightly, to his patrol car. As he walked between his apartment and our house, he turned a look of such malevolent hatred toward my window that I felt its impact and moved away into the safer darkness of the room. A sense of loss undefined, not known or understood, overcame me as I stood beside Linda. When she began to speak, I thought for a minute she was talking about Mark.

"Ella, I had to come home. He told me in Hot Springs (oh, Ella, he got so drunk). He was already married. All the time he whistled and smiled and sang those songs on my front porch, he was married. He sat down on the side of the bed in Hot Springs, took off his boots, and said he was married." Her face when she looked up at me, was filled with such hopelessness and despair that I had to look away.

"Linda, Linda, go to sleep," I told her. "You'll feel much better tomorrow." But her voice went on. Sitting limply on the side of the bed, only her hands moved, clasping and unclasping in her lap. Her voice, raspy and tired, seemed to come from the nape of her neck, suddenly too vulnerable, or from between her sagging, drooping shoulders, "Oh, Ella, I'd have stayed even then. Even then I'd have stayed but he laughed and said he'd never marry me. He said after the war, he'd go back to his wife in California. And I loved him and he never cared. He only laughed and he never cared."

I moved still farther away from my sister, saying politely, "Try to get a little sleep. You'll feel better tomorrow. We'll both feel better."

But I know we will not, for now we have come too close, and this closeness has made her a stranger. Her agony buried all those years beneath the tired order and monotonous trivia of our lives has returned and, for both of us, a new balance must be struck, a new repose must be found.

My Mother Had a Maid

In the East Texas town where I grew up there were two societies—one composed of the old, the unblemished (at least publicly so), the moneyed. The other was made up of those just below; that is, those who were faintly flawed, marred in some way by an unfortunate marriage or by the unsavory trade of a grandfather, long dead, or by a public flaunting of some community standard. The differences between the two societies were so minute, their shadings so subtle, that only those of us who lived there and who belonged to one or the other of those two societies could distinguish between them. And although it was never spoken of, certainly not by those in the highest echelon, nor even by those just below, the barrier—unassailable, invisible, impenetrable—was as apparent to those who belonged to one of these two societies as is a stone fence to a rider attempting to jump the fence.

I was reminded of this yesterday at the Country Club where I, on a visit to my last remaining relative, a great-aunt, had taken my young son, Robert V, for a swim. Although the town now has three country clubs, the one I refer to is, of course, the one built at the turn of the century by a lumber man, Lawrence Hudson, whose descendants still enjoy the revenue from vast holdings of timber in Arkansas, Louisiana and East Texas.

Driving past the modest gate posts which mark the entrance into the grounds, I was immediately conscious that here was a world of order. The narrow drive, curving gracefully for a mile or more, which is bordered by an excellent golf course on one side and on the other by magnificent pines (here, only nature is permitted such lavishness), leads one to the clubhouse, and here, too, there is the old, the established. The architecture is restrained and solid. The white wooden rockers on the wide verandah are ample, the ballroom floor is lightly polished, the chintzes on the sofas and chairs, gently faded.

Although I am now a great distance away from the Country Club, geographically and, I hope, psychologically, when I drove to the Club yesterday, there was a pleasant sense that I had in some manner regained or even returned to my rightful place in that quaint and beautiful town. Perhaps Cinco felt it, too, because he jumped right into the pool and immediately began diving for pennies with three other children, while I, a male invading, and very much aware that I was invading, the domain of women, ordered a beer and stood by the diving board, distancing myself from the three women in bathing suits who reclined in those wonderfully comfortable chairs at the shallow end of the pool, watching their offspring play with my son.

Seeing their tanned skins, their white teeth, their manicured nails, I thought of my wife. Totally without artifice (and comfortable in four languages), Rosemarie swims in the lakes

and seas of Europe and Indonesia. And thinking of her, I wondered what those women would see if she were here with me
and, also, what they now saw as they looked at me. Seeing a
blond-headed man as tanned as they, they'd first wonder who
he was, and who or what had brought him to their town.

The women had not recognized me. And how could they?
Both my teeth and my eyes had been straightened soon after we moved away, and now I was twenty years older and
as many pounds lighter. But from behind my dark glasses, I
had looked at the women long enough to remember who they
were. Margaret Carter had been a cheerleader. Today her swim
suit was red, but in her last year in high school she had almost
always worn white, a conceit she had begun, she confessed
to me one Christmas, after reading a single poem by Emily
Dickinson. The woman in the blue suit would be Lillian, the
daughter of a banker. Her hair golden and with those great,
blue eyes. And even in high school those enormous thighs. The
third woman, Mary Leigh, had been the daughter of a judge.
She had not been a pretty girl, but some other promise which
had been there had been fulfilled, and now she was attractive,
a woman to be noticed. These were the women who had been
chosen by—no, who had chosen—the football captains and
class presidents and valedictorians to go out with; women who
by virtue of their beauty and family and intelligence would
not have noticed me or even known my name had I not been a
damn good dancer.

Yesterday, as I watched my son in the pool, I had taken a
ridiculous pleasure in the way the three women straightened
themselves in their chairs, placing brown hands over stomachs
they tried to flatten whenever I glanced their way. When Cinco

came running up to ask if he could have a hot dog with the other children, I realized how stupid was my pretense at being a stranger. After all, twenty years is a long time, and now, meeting as adults, I would simply tell them who I was and enjoy their company for the short time Cinco and I would be at the club.

Sending Cinco to rejoin the children in the pool, I ordered a hot dog for him and then walked the length of the pool to where the women sat. Taking off my sunglasses, I extended my hand to Margaret, the woman I had known best.

"Hello, Maggie. I'm Robert Moore," I told her.

Frowning up at me, she put her hand over her eyes, making her hand a visor from the sun. "I'm not sure . . . ," she began.

But then Lillian touched her arm. "Why, Meg," she said hoarsely, "It's Bobby Joe. It's Bobby Joe Moore. You remember."

"Oh, Bobby Joe. Course I remember. Why I remember your whole family," Margaret said, and there was no doubting the genuine warmth in her voice. "Bobby Joe, I swear that every time Ernest and I get out on the dance floor, I wish for you. I really do."

"It's good to see the three of you. It's good to be home again," I told them. And, at that minute, with the sun on my back and the faint chlorine smell of the pool and the wide smiles of the three women, it *was* good to be home again.

Leaning forward, her breasts overflowing the full cups of her suit, Lillian said, "You make yourself a stranger, not coming home any more often than you do."

"Robert Moore, my law," Margaret said. "That cute little

boy must be yours. Is your wife—you are still married, aren't you—in town, too?"

The slight effrontery of her question sharpened my reply.

"Rosemarie doesn't enjoy East Texas," I said. "She's in Mexico with her family."

Margaret leaned back and raised her eyebrows. "Well, not everybody has to like East Texas," she said. "Lord, there have been times when I've wanted to leave here myself."

"After spending three months in London and Paris and I don't know where all last year, this town looked mighty good to me when I got back home," Lillian said. Her smile remained as she swept her hair up away from her neck. "So your wife is visiting her family in Mexico. I've never been to Mexico. From what everybody says, Mexico is so . . . ."

"Dirty?" I finished. Somewhat amused, I waited, knowing the question that hung in the air. I wondered which of the women would fancy herself with the subtlety to ask about the ethnicity of my wife.

"In Mexico," Mary Leigh echoed. "With her family."

The three looked at Cinco. *He is dark,* they would be thinking. *Not that it matters,* they would quickly add and later say to each other.

As we watched, one of the little boys splashed Cinco. The surprised, slightly anxious expression on his face tugged at my heart, but when he dove under the water and emerged laughing in a shower of sun-drenched spray, I relaxed.

Finally, it was Margaret, Margaret who had never said an unkind word about anybody all through high school, who found a way to ask.

"What's his name? What's your little boy's name?" she asked.

"He's named after me," I said, and some part of me was beginning to enjoy the game. I added, "We call him 'Cinco.'"

After a minute, "Cute," Lillian said, the word falling like gravel.

A waiter came from the clubhouse deftly carrying the children's lunch on a silver tray, and Mary Leigh rose from her chair and walked to the pool's edge. "You all get out now and come eat your hot dogs. And be nice to this little boy. His name's Cinco." Turning, she pulled the bottom of her suit away from her legs, snapping it smartly back in place. Her voice was warm. "I've wondered about you, Bobby Joe. The funniest thing. The day you left, the *very* day, Rufus had gone to pick up our mail at the station, and he told us you had boarded the afternoon train, going east. I remember because it was the day, the *very* day after that maid of yours . . . ." Fiddling with the right strap of her yellow suit, she gazed at me, wide-eyed.

All at once the years fell away and the past—the small ring beside the folded newspaper, a gold star, the smell of gasoline—was before me. Shaken, I told the women that by now Aunt Emily would be wondering what had happened to me, and got Cinco, protesting, out of the pool.

Driving to Aunt Emily's house afterwards, dimly aware of Cinco's complaints about his abandoned hot dog, I was dismayed by the pain I had felt during my brief encounter with the three—good-hearted, most would say—women. I had returned home for the first time when my father had died, but after that only when my presence had been made necessary by Anne's illness and most recently by her death. Now I had brought Cinco home to Aunt Emily, the last of the "Little Brontës," as the town affectionately referred to them. Charlotte, my grandmother, had died soon after my father's birth, leaving his rearing to an indifferent father and to the remaining aunts. Anne had survived well into her eighties, apparently relishing her spinsterhood. But now there was only Emily who, although twice married, had been a widow most of her life. My great affection for her had always been returned, I felt, in like measure. And when she had written: "*I want you to bring Robert home. The child needs his people, and, Lord knows, I need him,*" I immediately planned the trip home.

It seems to me that we all have two homes: the first is the house in which we are reared and the second is the one where our children grow up. Now I had returned to my first home, or rather to its memory, for shortly after my father's death the house was gone.

Twenty years ago. Her name was Barbara, and I was seventeen. Because of the war a high turnover of domestic employees had begun. Maids came and went with surprising frequency—to join their husbands at an army camp, to take a job in a munitions factory. "Out the back door and gone before they have a chance to learn our ways," my father would say.

"Why work for white folks," Mother might answer, "when they can make three times as much as a cook at the Lone Star Defense Plant.

Even before the new maid had come to work for us, Mother must have seemed unfathomable to her husband. Gazing at her, his brow slightly furrowed, "Barbara, I declare, you sound like you're . . . one of them."

My mother would throw back her head and laugh. "Well, I'm pretty dark," she might reply, her eyes glistening with humor.

I would look at my father, hoping to see the slight smile that would signal his capitulation to Mother's good spirits, but at such times my father effortlessly resisted what he called Mother's frivolous nature. Shaking his head, "Barbara, Barbara," he'd say in gentle remonstration.

Twenty years ago. In the middle of World War II. With an early October chill in the air, the kitchen was cold and, drawn by the rays of the sun, I had come outside to sit on the steps and wait for the new maid to show up and fix breakfast. And when I heard her whistling, I thought it was the iceman, whistling, but no, it was the maid. Barefooted, swinging her shoes in her right hand, she seemed to sway, rather than walk, up the winding drive. Wearing a blue cotton dress, the sun glistening on her gold earrings and gold necklace, she whistled right up to the steps. When she smiled down at me, the star-shaped gold filling in her front tooth shone like a jewel. Unexpected.

"You Bobby," she said. "Well, I'm yore mama's new maid."

Sitting beside me, she brushed the dust off her feet and slipped them into her shoes. "Got to protect these shoes from road wear," she said. "Sold my last shoe stamps before I went to California to tell my honey goodbye. Rode all the way barefooted. Didn't put my shoes on 'til San Diego. Got off the train looking good. Sure did now." A note of pleasure in her voice, she fingered the silver ring she wore. Then she put her elbows on the step behind her and lifted her face to the sun. "I just about didn't come to work this morning. I'd rather a stayed home in my husband's arms, but he done left. On a ship. Going somewhere." The gold star, twinkling, belied the sadness in her voice.

I had no idea how to reply. I had never thought about a maid being in her husband's arms or even considered that a maid might have a husband. If I had thought of a colored's sexuality at all, it would have been in the context of literature: a cruel plantation owner having his way with a young, colored girl; a faithful retainer saving a white girl from a carpetbagger. In my mind maids seemed no more than female eunuchs, but now here was my mother's new maid, talking about staying in the arms of her husband, *in bed* in the arms of her husband.

She did not seem to be in any hurry to cook my breakfast, and there was nothing I could do but wait. Ordinarily, not even my father would ask a maid to perform a task. If I or my sister or even my father wanted something done, one of us would tell Mother, and she would ask the maid to do it. After all, she was my mother's maid.

Throwing a quick glance her way, I saw within the mysterious confines of her blue dress the edge of a red brassiere and above it the curve of a dark breast. *Oh, Lord,* I thought.

"What's your name?" I asked, dismayed by the squeak in my voice.

"Barbara."

"Why, that's my mother's name! Her name's Barbara!"

"No law against two," she said comfortably. "I'm Barbara Conner."

Another first. A maid with a last name.

She stood and stretched, slowly raising her shoulders, rolling them back, like a cat, straining the cotton fabric across her breasts, revealing nipples the size of nickels.

She smiled. *Does she know? Could she?* I wondered. I crossed my arms over my lap.

"Well, I reckon I'll get on inside and heat up the stove, see if I can cook you some buttermilk pancakes. You reckon you all got the fixings for that?"

In a few minutes she had the stove going, the kitchen warm, the plates heating on the pilot light, and pretty soon she was placing a stack of pancakes and a pitcher of maple syrup on the table in front of me. Knowing before I took a bite how good they were going to taste, I spread the slowly melting butter over the pancakes and bathed them in maple syrup. She had retreated and was standing, arms crossed, by the kitchen window. Outside on the steps, she had seemed small, but now I saw that she was tall, every bit as tall as Mother. She was also just as slender. At the sound of water running into Father's bath tub, she looked toward the ceiling. Her neck was unusually long, like a dancer's.

"Reckon that means somebody else will be down here pretty soon. Yore mama or yore daddy?"

"My mother doesn't eat breakfast. And you don't have to worry about Celia's. When my father honks, she'll run downstairs and grab a piece of toast so she can be out of the house and in the car before he honks again." The maid took a plate from the stove and came toward the table. *Will it seem like I'm correcting her? What I am about to say?* "My dad doesn't eat in the kitchen. He likes peace and quiet while he reads his paper."

"Reckon I'll just wait then. He can tell me what he wants."

Except for Celia's hurried footsteps and my father's more leisurely paced ones, all was quite upstairs. Two or three times a week Celia had a small crisis. Over her hair: "I can't stand it!" she'd cry, this followed by Mother's voice as she took the brush and persuaded both Celia and her hair that all was well. Or, "I haven't a thing to wear!" she'd wail and Mother, cajoling, "What about my new cashmere with your blue skirt?"

I buttered another pancake. A mockingbird began its extravagant song. I heard my father's footsteps coming down the stairs. Clean-shaven and gray-suited, he came briskly into the kitchen. Holding his jacket over his shoulder with his index finger, he sounded hopeful. "So you're Mrs. Moore's new maid. What's your name?"

"Barbara." Her smile is wide.

He frowned, tilted his head to the side. "Barbara," he said, puzzled. "But Mrs. Moore's name is Barbara." His frown deepened. "Well, she'll work all that out." A slight smile flickered at the corners of his mouth. "The truth is I smelled those damn pancakes and that got me up and going. You reckon you can cook up a stack for me?"

But the new maid was already pouring batter into one skillet, frying sausage in another and handing him a cup of coffee. "I be making apricot preserves to go with some homemade bread after while. Have it ready for yore breakfast in the morning. Sure will now." Carrying a pot of coffee in one hand and the golden pancakes in the other, with her hip she pushed open the swinging door between the kitchen and the dining room.

"I'll just eat in here this morning. Keep Bobby company." Father rubbed his hands together, pulled a chair away from the table.

She nodded. "That way the pancakes still be hot when they gets to the table."

My father never ate in the kitchen. Suddenly the day was filled with possibility. The war would end, his business would improve, Mother would like living in the South.

"I've never known a girl to catch on so fast," Father said the next day and the day after. And said to his wife a few days later at the dinner table. "Barbara, this new girl will give you more time to get into things."

"Get into things?" Distastefully she stirred her coffee, added cream.

My father retreated. A little. "You know, help Celia. With the house running smoothly, you might plan a little party for Celia's friends. A Christmas party. Just yesterday the Little Brontes remarked that the Christmas season would begin soon."

Mother sighed, a long, shuddering sigh that suggested a terminal illness or some other impending disaster. She removed the gold ring on her finger, gazed at it, and replaced it.

"Robert, Celia's too young to be pushed into all this debutante business. It seems quite unnecessary."

"Unnecessary?" He was genuinely puzzled.

"With the war going on. You know the minute Bobby's eighteen they'll take him. Even with his eyesight. They're taking everybody now."

"Dad, I'm ready *now*. I want to get in there and get it over with. Leroy Elkins joined the army last week. His father signed the papers."

Her eyes filled. "Oh, Bobby."

"How in the hell did we get on this subject!" My father's face was slightly flushed; his voice was raised. "We're talking about a little Christmas party for Celia and her friends. We're not talking about the war, for God's sake, excuse me Barbara." He clamped his lips together. A muscle on the right side of his face tightened. "Celia has to live here after all, and somebody has to help her."

Mother's heart was ardent, always, and easily moved by frailty or sorrow. Looking back, it seems as if she was forever trying to right some unknowable wrong that had been done my father or heal some grievous wound he had suffered— suffered, perhaps, as a result of his being a motherless child. For always, when I was crossways with him, "Remember, Bobby," she would say, "your father never had a mother."

Whatever the reason, at dinner that night her righteousness dissolved into pity. She reached across the table and took his hand and held it against her cheek. She kissed it.

My father played his trump card. "You know the Little Brontes love the children, and they love you too. They'll help. It hasn't been that long since they went through this."

"I'll call them," she promised.

Oh, this mother of mine. Unlike any other. At once the source of my greatest pride, my most abject despair. I was painfully aware that my friends, jabbing elbows into each other's ribs, falling onto the living room rug in exaggerated excitement whenever she left the room, noticed her loosely bound bosoms and saw the sway of her hips, although in my presence, they dared only remark on her long hair, as unconfined as her bosoms. But she was as indifferent to their crazy teenage admiration as she was to my embarrassment over it, as indifferent as she was to the ladies' Friday afternoon bridge parties and to the Sunday tea dances at the Club. While the other mothers carefully counted their tricks and politely tallied their scores at bridge, my mother was teeing off, usually by herself, or worse yet, suited out and swimming laps in the pool.

In the early years of marriage, my father gently urging, would say, "Don't you enjoy their company? Wouldn't you enjoy sitting with them and watching our children swim."

And she, a newcomer, ("*Your mother's a Yankee!*" Butch Henderson had called out when I was in first grade, the other children taking it up, crying, *Yankee, Yankee, Yankee!),* would answer, "Oh, Robert. It's tiresome. All that talk about lazy maids and bridge hands when the whole country is in the middle of a depression."

But, now, she invited the aunts to tea, an Irish tea. Hot scones with cream and apricot preserves her new maid had cooked. The aunts made suggestions, at first hesitantly. "Do you think Celia would enjoy ballroom dancing lessons? This is the time to learn," Anne said. "Then at Christmas a little party for her friends. A tea dance. At the Club."

Emily, twice-widowed and financially sound, loved the idea of a party, especially one that would please my father. "Or what about a Mardi Gras ball later in the season. Celia will be sixteen then. It would be a masque party. Young people love costumes." She took a hot scone, split it and spooned apricot preserves into it.

Anne nodded. "That would give us more time. We'll have to go to Neiman's for her dress."

My mother leaned back in her chair and splayed her legs out before her, deliberately evoking raised eyebrows. "What about a hunt breakfast? We could ship the horses in from Virginia."

After a minute, the Little Brontes smiled and pulled their chairs close. "Now Barbara, be serious."

She pulled her mane of black hair forward over her shoulder, sat straight in her chair, feet together, the very picture of compliance. "Let's make a list," she said.

After dinner, she read the list. The aunts beamed. Her husband was confounded. "My God, excuse me Barbara, that would cost a fortune!"

She smiled and reached for his hand. "We'll have Celia's party here. At the house. With lots of flowers and good food and somebody in to help Barbara. And a piano player."

Celia burst into tears. "I'd be so embarrassed! Nobody has parties at their house. Nobody will come. Nobody! If I can't have a party at the Club, I just won't have a party at all!" She stormed out of the room.

"Barbara, Celia's still not strong," my father reminded her. Since Celia's rheumatic fever we always tried not to upset her.

The Little Brontes agreed. The party must be at the Club.

After this a kind of serenity descended upon our household. The kitchen was filled with the sound of Barbara whisking egg whites into airy mounds for vanilla flavored custard and shucking sweet corn and filled, too, with the smell of corn bread and ham baking in the oven. And the maid's whistling. "Though there's one engine gone, we will still carry on," she whistled cheerfully. "Coming in on a wing and a prayer."

After school I cruised through the kitchen, lifting the tops of stove vessels to see what dinner would bring. "Have you

heard from . . . " *What to call this man I imagine as always in
her bed. Your soldier? Mister Conner? Mister?* Barbara waited,
hands on her hips. " . . . your husband," I finished.

She beamed and the gold star sparkled. "Yessir. Got a letter yesterday." She patted her apron pocket. "Read it so many
times I knows it by heart. Want to hear it?" When I nodded,
"Bobby, you set here and shuck this corn for Barbara, and I'll
say it for you. You got time?"

The other Barbara (I had begun to call her this) sat across
the table and each of us took up a roasting ear. She recited:

*My sweet woman, they give me a gun yesterday, a rifle.
Before that I just been bringing supplies back and forth, back
and forth. I reckon the white boys seen they need all the firepow-
er they can get and they handed me this gun. "Can you shoot?"
the man said. I shot the limb off a tree and he nodded and left
in his jeep. Some say we'll fight over here and some say across
the river, but as for me I just wants to get home to you, my sweet
honey.*

She ruffled my hair and laughed. "You too young for the
rest."

My father began to take his breakfast in the kitchen, eating
silently, saying only "Good morning, Barbara," and when he
finished, "Thank you, Barbara." But he frequently praised her
to Mother. "Barbara, ask your maid to make some more bread
pudding. Until she served it last week, I thought the making of
bread pudding was a lost art."

In October, Celia, accompanied by the aunts, drove to
Dallas to choose a dress. "Barbara, don't you want to go? The
child might need your advice about a dress," my father said.

"No, dear. The aunts have insisted the dress will be a gift.

Knowing Celia, I'm afraid she'll show no mercy when it comes to cost. Of time or money. Robert, it does seem so foolish to spend all this money. Things haven't been going well at the store. You're not sleeping well. And with the war, this is not the time . . . ."

He cupped her chin in his hand. "Now don't you worry about money. That's my job."

She brushed his hand away. "Oh, Robert," she said despairingly.

That afternoon Wayne Schuster, who by working for his father and carrying two paper routes had managed to buy an old Chevy, gave me a ride home. Turning into the driveway, I saw the two women sitting on the back steps, barefooted, their skirts hiked above their knees to catch any breeze that might come their way. Mother was almost as dark as the other Barbara and from this distance, coming upon them, they might have been sisters. As we watched, Mother, overtaken with mirth, threw her head back and slapped her thigh, and the other Barbara, with a hand on each knee, laughed along with Mother, a rollicking laugh that bounced through the open windows of the Chevy.

"Why, that's your mother!" Wayne said.

"So? Want to make something of it?" My fist was in his face, threatening him, and he drew back, astonished. I slammed the car door, and Wayne took off, squealing his tires around the corner.

As I stalked across the yard, Mother said, "Oh, Bobby, Barbara just told me the funniest joke about Hitler. A colored man went up to . . . ."

She stopped when she saw my face, and I stormed into the

house without a word to the other Barbara. Throwing myself on my bed, I could hear Mother's voice, sounding not at all disturbed, blending with her maid's.

I lay there, willing my father to come. I *wanted* him to see them. I wanted him to *do* something. But when I heard his car in the drive, my stomach tightened. I got up and went to the window. Dad closed the car door and walked quickly across the lawn. "Mrs. Moore, come inside, please," he said.

Our family was often divided into two camps. I identified with my mother. As I saw it, we were both outcasts—I, because of my lazy eye and my acne and, also (I felt this acutely at times), because of my mother. She was from the north—a Yankee, a newcomer, continually flaunting the mores and customs of the town.

Now, hearing my father's voice, iced by controlled fury, I had an inkling of his humiliation. We had, as they say, come down in the world, come down in that small East Texas world. But it was only a monetary decline. We still had family—the two aunts, who were beyond reproach, and we had my father's ancestors—a great-grandfather who had been a Texas congressman and a great-great aunt who had become the fifty-three-year-old bride of a man who had once been the governor of Texas. But in that one brief moment in Wayne Schuster's car I saw that Mother was hastening our downfall. And I knew that she did not care. For the first time, I felt vindicated as I listened to my father's angry voice.

"Barbara, sitting out there, barefooted, for all the world to see! And with your skirt hiked up over your head! Dammit! Barbara!"

And for the first time his use of a curse word in Mother's presence was not followed by an apology.

Hearing Mother's soft knock on my door that night, I remained silent, my eyes fixed on my open book. She came in and sat on the edge of my bed. I kept my eyes on the book. She took it from my hand, placed a book marker in it and closed it.

"Bobby?"

"Mother, he's right! You did look like a maid this afternoon. Wayne Schuster was shocked. I was humiliated."

"Oh, Bobby. You and Wayne Schuster! You don't even know that there's a world out there, and there's a war being fought in that world! Well, you'll soon find out there's more to be shocked about than your mother sitting on the back steps with the best damn, excuse me, Bobby, as your father would say, maid we've ever had!" The ice that had been in my father's voice when he spoke to Mother had traversed into hers as she spoke to me. Stung into silence, I did not answer and after a minute she left the room.

Now, my father, although he dared not fire Mother's maid, found a dozen reasons for her dismissal. Mother found a hundred reasons to keep her. Under my father's polite, remorseless siege, I found myself again allied with Mother.

Once again, my father had his breakfast served in the dining room where he rarely spoke to the maid. And she went heavily about her tasks, sighing often. She refused to make my father's favorites—bread pudding (takes too much sugar), fried okra (too much bacon grease). In the war that was being waged she was heart and soul on Mother's side.

I was changing a tire the day I heard the other Barbara ask Mother for money. "I hates to ask. I surely does. You got so much on you right now, but Doctor Bruce he say I need to have this knot out, and he has to have the money for the procedure."

Mother put her arm around her maid's shoulders. "Oh, I am sorry. Does it hurt?" Her voice was full of compassion.

"No'am. But he say it will."

"Of course you can have the money. I'll speak to Mr. Moore tonight. How much does Doctor Bruce need?"

"He say fifty now and fifty later."

"I'll speak to my husband tonight."

Throughout the war, at precisely six-thirty, maids from households all over town would slip into the falling darkness, allowing back screen doors to whisper to a close behind them, and the town would prepare to listen to the news. All activity would cease and chairs would be drawn close to the radio. My father would settle into his leather chair, Mother would take the rocker, and I would sit on the floor to be as close to the news as possible.

This night Walter Winchell began as usual: "Good-evening, Mr. and Mrs. North America and all the ships at sea. It's bad news tonight. In the Ardennes the Germans have breached our defenses and are only one hundred miles from Antwerp. If the U.S. Defense . . . ."

Mother stood and turned off the radio.

"Barbara!" my father said.

"Robert, our maid needs money for surgery. It's quite serious."

"Where does she plan to get this money?"

"Why Robert, from us, of course."

Rising from his chair, he slapped a folded newspaper against his leg. "It's out of the question."

Mother's hands were outstretched. "You can't refuse."

"Our expenses are heavy. I don't have it. Barbara, you know what the war has done to my business. You've been in the store."

"I know how much we're spending on Celia's Christmas party."

"That is totally irrelevant."

"Not to me."

With a final *whack* against his leg, and "No, Barbara. And that's final," he left the room.

Seeing the shocked disbelief on Mother's face, I longed to be able to give her the money.

The next morning Mother, still in her pink gown and robe, was down before my father. "Barbara, I'm going to work something out today. You tell Dr. Bruce to schedule the surgery."

The other Barbara turned from the sink, her shoulder blades wings beneath her yellow dress. "I thank you, Miss Barbara. And I wrote my sweetie. He'll send the money for it. He surely will." Leaning against the icebox, she clasped her hands beneath her chin. "Trouble is, I ain't heard lately. Nothing. And last night I had this dream." Her voice was mournful, almost keening. "He wore dead in my dream, on the ship. Now his spirit got to haunt the ship." She shook her head repeatedly as if denying her dream.

"Barbara, there's no such thing as a ghost. It was just a

dream. You'll hear from him soon. Try not to worry." Mother turned to leave, turned back. "And, Barbara, we won't mention the surgery to anyone," she said, before hurrying upstairs. The other Barbara understood as well as I that by *anyone* she meant my father.

I know, as well as if I had been there, what must have happened at the jeweler's that morning. Mother, her head held high, would have walked into the store, removed the ring from her finger and placed it carelessly on the square of black velvet. She would then have taken from her purse the diamond that had belonged to her mother and placed it beside her wedding band. "Dick, I want to sell one of my rings," she said. "Whichever will bring a hundred dollars."

Now Mother knew that Dick Morris was one of my father's oldest friends. Their friendship, begun in Miss Elam's Day School when they were five, had sustained itself by virtue of age. Although they seldom saw each other, on social occasions such as a christening or a funeral or a wedding, Dick Morris was always in attendance. "I can count on old Dick to be there when he's needed," Father was fond of saying.

In Dick's mind, being confronted with Mother's rings on the black velvet square would have seemed an occasion amounting to a crisis. He would have contrived a courteous excuse to leave Mother's presence, leaving her unsuspecting, and hurried to his office to call Father. I've always wondered what he said, what he *could* have said to my father. And what would have been his tone—cajoling? amused? sympathetic? when he said it? But I know, because the other Barbara told me, that when he and Mother returned to the house about noon, he opened the car door for her, escorted her to the house and, without a word, drove back to his office. Mother went immediately upstairs. There she moved his things from her room to the guest room at the end of the hall.

When I came from school, Mother and the other Barbara were again on the back steps. Today their dresses, Mother's best navy blue and Barbara's familiar yellow, were tucked demurely below their knees. Mother's face was pale, her expression serious, her grief palpable. I spoke, and they replied. But then they were silent, waiting to resume their conversation when I had left.

But as I entered the house, I did hear Mother: "Oh, Barbara, with this terrible, heartbreaking war, the hardware business is difficult. But, tell Dr. Bruce that we . . . ." I am sure she said "we," and that was all I heard.

Mother's maid did not come to work on Monday. On Tuesday, a glimmer of gold on the dining table caused me to veer from my path to the kitchen. Mother's gold ring lay beside Father's folded newspaper. Gazing down at the ring and at Father's carefully folded paper, I sensed the emotional storm that was about to engulf our family. But it never occurred to me that the other Barbara would be at the eye of the storm.

Our maid was gone a week. If Mother knew the reason for her absence, she did not say. Father never asked. We came down to a cold kitchen and had cold cereal and left the house as soon as we could. Father continued to use the room across the hall, and only one time did he knock on Mother's door. It was in the early morning hours. "Barbara," he called softly. "Barbara, please." If she answered, I did not hear her.

A week later, the other Barbara returned to work. When I came down and saw her at the kitchen sink, my heart lifted. "Barbara!" I said. "Here you are! You're back!"

She nodded and smiled (such a small smile), her lips curling around her teeth. "What you want for breakfast?"

"Barbara, I don't care. But where have you been? I've missed you. Mother's missed you, too. I know she has," I said, believing still that all would be well.

"I be all right, right soon," she said. "Done had my procedure."

It was when she stooped to get the iron skillet from a stove drawer that she grimaced, and I saw the gaping hole where her gold-star tooth had been. "Oh, Barbara!" I said, shocked by the change in her appearance.

She covered her mouth with her hand. "Ain't nothing to be done about it," she said. Placing my breakfast before me, she touched my shoulder. "It all right, Bobby. Just a tooth."

"No. It's not all right," Mother said softly. Neither of us had heard her come down. Wearing the velvet robe Father had given her on her birthday, she stood, with her hands in the pockets, her chin thrust forward. "Barbara, I'm glad you're back. We've missed you. We'll have a little visit after breakfast."

At Celia's wail, "Mother, I can't find my red sweater!" she turned to go back upstairs just as Father came down. "Robert, Barbara's back. She had her surgery. She sold her gold star tooth to pay for it," she said, speaking as if to a stranger.

"I knew she would work it out," he said reasonably.

"Robert, I never intend to be placed in that position again."

The next day she was dressed before we left for school. She

dressed early the next day and the next. The following Monday, Judge Baker, my father's first cousin once removed, stopped by the hardware store for "a little visit."

Father could not contain his rage when he entered the house that evening. "Goddamnit, Barbara, do you know what you're doing to me?" he shouted, not caring that Celia and I could hear every word. "Going all over town, looking for a job. As if a man can't take care of his family. I don't understand you, Barbara. What in God's name do you want?"

"Robert, you really don't know, do you? You haven't any idea," she said, a sad wonder in her voice.

That afternoon her maid helped Mother pack. "Miss Barbara, all this here ain't necessary. It wore just a tooth," she said.

"It's more than a tooth, Barbara. It's much more than a tooth."

Later that afternoon, I heard them laughing, giggling like schoolgirls. *Maybe she's not going to leave us,* I thought. I knocked on the door.

"Come in, Bobby," Mother called cheerfully. "We're talking about ghosts. This girl believes in ghosts. Tell him, Barbara."

"I has to haunt the house where I passes. All us coloreds knows it." So caught up was she in the telling that for the first time she forgot to cover her mouth. "All I wants is for yore mama to say that if I dies here, here in this house, she be here too. With me."

"Oh, Barbara, you're not going to die," Mother said.

"I has to haunt the house where I dies, and I don't want no strangers round. I wants them I knows. If I passes here, you got to come back."

"But you are not going to die," Mother said. "Your sweetie will come home from the war, and you'll live happily ever after." Mother, excited by what she was about to do, was taking her clothes from hangers and tossing them on the bed for her maid to pack.

"I got to know."

"All right, I promise," Mother said gaily.

When she was packed, I took her bags downstairs, and she called a taxi. When she came down, she made her hand into a fist and touched my chin. "Bobby, you're a man now," she said. "But I want you to promise you'll wait to be drafted. Don't join the army. Promise? Will you promise?"

In our family, promises were not given lightly. Dismayed by what she asked, I shook my head. "Oh, Mother," I said. But then she looked so stricken that I said, "I'll wait. I promise."

Talking to herself, the other Barbara came slowly down the stairs. "A tooth don't matter," she muttered. "You'd think Hitler had come in here on us. Or that gorilla had caught Ma Perkins. A tooth ain't nothing." She started to the kitchen.

"Wait a minute, Barbara," Mother said. "I want a promise from you, too."

"Yes ma'am." She turned and came back, her face alive with eagerness to promise anything, everything.

"I want you to find enough sugar to make bread pudding for Mr. Moore. Will you?"

The other Barbara frowned.

Mother chuckled. "Promise. I want your promise."

"I will," her maid said solemnly. "And now I got to see what I can find for supper. I don't hold with good-byes."

All that afternoon Celia had refused to come out of her

room, but now she stormed out, sobbing, throwing herself into Mother's arms, begging her to stay. And when Mother refused, she made a frantic telephone call to our father. But he could not stop her. Somehow, perhaps from Aunt Emily, she had the money for her ticket.

After Mother left, Barbara continued to work for us, becoming thin and stooped as the weeks passed, growing old before our eyes. I don't know why she stayed on. Perhaps, she did not have the energy to find another job, or perhaps she hoped Mother would return. Just after Christmas a telegram came, and a gold star was hung in the house of her husband's mother. But she said nothing about her husband's death to us. She came to work, trudging determinedly up the drive, almost every day. Several times I found her hunched over in the kitchen, her face gray and glistening with perspiration. Once, her voice a whisper, she said, "Bobby, my medication. In my handbag. And bring old Barbara some water."

I hurried to do as she had asked. And when the pain receded, she patted my hand. "You a good boy, Bobby," she said.

I wrote Mother then and asked her to come home. She replied, saying she felt her work in Washington was useful to the war effort.

On a cold Friday in February, the teachers had a planning day, and the school was closed. I stopped by the house to pick up my golf clubs and change clothes. When I saw Barbara, wraith-like, dragging herself and a gas can up the back steps, I thought she was doing some special cleaning. "Don't work too hard," I called, but she did not hear me. *Oh, the sky was blue that day, the air so clear it pierced the heart.* I got my clubs out of the garage and started into the house. Then I smelled the fumes, heard the *poof* of the explosion, called her name. I saw her. Engulfed in flames, she sat in a kitchen chair, her mouth open in a silent cry of anguish, her hands raised in helpless supplication.

I yelled to a passing car and ran for the garden hose. But she was dead before I could drag the hose into the kitchen.

The fire department came so fast that only a circle around the kitchen chair was damaged. "What in the world could that nigger have been thinking of?" the fireman said. "Why, she could have burned your house to the ground!"

The next day I caught a train to Washington, and I lived there with Mother until I was drafted. Celia chose to stay with our father and the Little Brontes. When the war ended, I was on a ship in the South Pacific, never having fired a shot in combat.

Mother kept her promise to her maid. And perhaps she felt some pity, some affection for her husband. At any rate, when I was drafted, she came home and lived with Father until he died, quite suddenly, ten years after the war's end. When the house was struck by lightening and burned to the ground, Mother, released from her promise to her maid, went back to Washington and lives there still, an adoring grandmother and a loving, gentle mother to me and Rosemarie when she visits. She has never spoken of that sad time.

After a week with Aunt Emily, Cinco and I rejoined Rosemarie in Mexico. My first evening at home, we had one of those perfect dinners—leisurely and beautiful with good food and wine and candlelight—that spring from the joy of reunion. After dinner we sat on the balcony and I, stirred by old memories, carefully recounted those last months and weeks of that other Barbara's life to my wife. "Poor things," she said, when I had finished. "Poor things." And later that night, she took her worn Shakespeare from our library and read to me that haunting passage, the one that begins, "My mother had a maid called Barbara" and ends: "She had a song of willow / And she died singing it."

Afterword

A short story. These short stories. I have no idea why a particular image or phrase or gesture or encounter becomes a short story. Why not a chapter in a novel? Or a poem? Before I write anything, anything at all, I begin each day by reading poetry. Just now it is Yeats. When I am transported by the power and beauty of "The Lake Isle of Innisfree," for example, I can begin my day of writing with energy and a sense of ease.

Short stories come from conscious or subconscious memories. A writer holds a particular memory in her mind as she might choose a pebble to hold in the palm (I love the word, *palm*) of her hand. She turns it over and over, smoothing it, discovering its colors, finding its jagged edges and then puts it away until . . . there! There it is again, in her hand. And she must do something with it, do *something* by reliving the memory; that is, by trying to understand it or to accept it or to laugh at it. Finally, after much vision and revision, these lively little pebbles become short stories.

Some years ago, on a flight to Santa Fe, I found myself in a nest of story-telling southerners who seemed to be on a first

name basis with all the southern writers. They spoke intimately of Faulkner, calling him Bill, and said Tennessee Williams'
brother swore he had been murdered and said that when Miss
Welty got behind the wheel of her car in Jackson, everything—
chickens and vehicles and pedestrians—scattered. A man from
Georgia had been standing in the aisle, arms crossed, listening, nodding, smiling. Then, speaking slowly and deliberately
so that each word seemed full of import, "Jane," he said, "I'm
pretty sure I saw Flannery's last peacock get hit by a red pickup
truck."

"I'm going to write a story about that," I told him, and
years later I did. My story began with the sentence, "Duffy was
a man." I had no idea how it was going to get there, but I knew
precisely where it was headed, and the next day I changed one
word. "Duffy was a thief," I wrote and, after that, one sentence
followed upon the heels of another so that the story seemed to
write itself.

I was signing *A Place Called Sweet Shrub* in a bookstore
in Shreveport, Louisiana, when a woman wearing a silk dress
with a red belt walked up to the table, picked up a book and
said, "What's this about?" This question is the most common
and the most difficult a writer is asked. Stumbling around I
said, "It's about love." Sighing, she examined the book jacket
cover. In an attempt to ratchet up her interest, I added: "It's
about taking chances." But clearly, she wasn't one to throw her
bonnet over the windmill, as my grandmother used to say. "Is
it a mystery?" she asked hopefully. "No," I said. "But it culmi-
nates in one of the most violent race riots we've ever had in this
country."

She threw the book down on the table. "I wouldn't read

this book if you gave it to me!" she said vehemently. "Not after what happened to my mother!" she added and hurried to leave the store.

Astonished, I said, "Wait! What happened to your mother?"

She turned around, came back, flattened her hands on the table and leaned toward me. "Three weeks ago," she said angrily, "her maid came to work, sat down at the kitchen table, poured gasoline on herself, and set herself on fire." Then she rushed from the store, leaving me stunned and silent. Years later I wrote "My Mother Had a Maid," about that encounter, solving the *how's* and *why's* and *where's* of it imaginatively and satisfactorily.

Writing the story called "The Dress" was a great comfort. Its origin was a fairly recent television news story about a little girl who had been kidnapped by a stranger. The man who had kidnapped her was all over the convenience store, but the little girl he had kidnapped remained frozen in place, arms crossed, beseechingly looking up at the faces of the grownups who walked by her. "Help me! Please help me," she silently pled, with her unnaturally still posture, her little folded arms, her upturned face. The video from the convenience store was broadcast repeatedly, and each time I watched it I told myself I would have noticed, I would have paid attention, I would have helped her. In writing "The Dress," I stepped into the story and baked gingerbread (I don't bake), made a dress (I can't sew), and rocked the little girl.

"Beneath the Jacaranda" was written years after my sister and I spent a summer water coloring and writing under a blossoming jacaranda tree in San Miguel de Allende. When I transplanted the tree to Dallas and put a nude woman with blue eyes under it, the story came alive. The pebble with which "Spurs That Jangle" began was the memory of a young woman, who had dated a soldier for twelve years, who came home alone after a marriage that lasted twelve days. If my family knew what had happened between the two, they never told me. This past September I went to the East Texas Book Festival in Tyler. That first evening I went to the drugstore to buy (I always forget something) a tooth brush and toothpaste. A young woman stood behind the cash register. As she made the transaction, her gestures were so tender and the words she spoke were so startling that the encounter seems beyond the telling. But its memory is now in the palm of my hand. I'll write about it. Someday.

JANE ROBERTS WOOD
Argyle, Texas

Seven Stories was designed and composed by Kellye Sanford
in Minion Pro open type, 11.25 point on 16 point leading.
Minion Pro Italic was selected for display.
Printed in an edition of 1000 copies
by Edwards Brothers, Ann Arbor, Michigan.